To Joan Koshela,
Thank you!
Mark Griffin
Jeanne Siegrist

Good Night, Dear Hart, Good Night

Good Night, Dear Hart, Good Night

The Untold Story of Hart Lester Allen
and
Her Connection to the Infamous
Charles Ponzi

Jeannie Gionfriddo
&
Mark Gionfriddo

Epigraph Books
Rhinebeck, New York

Good Night, Dear Hart, Good Night: The Untold Story of Hart Lester Allen and Her Connection to the Infamous Charles Ponzi © 2016 by Jeannie Gionfriddo & Mark Gionfriddo

All rights reserved. No part of this book may be used or reproduced in any manner without written permission from the author except in reviews and critical articles. Contact the publisher for information.

Paperback ISBN: 978-1-944037-33-8
Hardcover ISBN: 978-1-944037-34-5
Library of Congress Control Number: 2016943786

Epigraph Books
22 East Market Street, Suite 304
Rhinebeck, NY 12572
(845) 876.4861
www.epigraphps.com

Printed in the United States of America.

Prologue

It was a cold, windy morning as our small procession of cars silently rolled through the cemetery. Tall pines lined the road like silent guards keeping vigil. The road wound down into a secluded valley, the grassy slopes on each side housing several old mausoleums. To the right of a grassy area stood a huge statue of a man. As we slowly drove past, the name "DANIEL HARRIS" leapt out in large letters.

The limousines stopped, as did the other vehicles following. As I stepped out, I heard the loud thud of car doors being slammed as others exited their vehicles. The wind pulled at my coat as I looked around and thought what a fitting place this was to put our dear Hart to rest. Surrounded by her parents and siblings, it was such a peaceful setting.

As we followed the minister up the grass covered hill and gathered around the casket, I noticed there was just a handful of people present. At ninety-two, Hart had outlived most of her family and friends. I stifled a sob and felt as if my heart would break, for Hart and I had become so close. She had accepted me as the daughter she never had, and I her, as the mother I had lost so many years ago. Gazing around, I understood why Hart was so adamant on being buried here in this beautiful section of the cemetery. The tall trees reached high into the blue sky, and the serene setting made it a lovely haven. I looked at the casket and I remembered the small, worn poem I had found tucked away between the pages of her Bible:

> Oh, summer sun, shine warmly here;
> Oh, eastern wind, blow softly here;
> Green sward above, lie light, lie light;
> Good night, dear heart, good night, good night...

Chapter 1

On an afternoon in December of 1920 in the heart of Boston, the full brunt of the incredible Ponzi scandal lay heavily on everyone's mind. The bitter aftertaste of greed and avarice filled the mouths of the investors duped by the charming but oh-so-cunning Charles Ponzi. Ponzi—a name that would go down in history as one of the biggest con artists of all time, yet, strangely enough, a kind of hero to many. Thousands of sheep were led to slaughter, yet some still believed in him, and blamed others for the fall of his "great plan." Hart Allen's husband Joe was one of those unfortunates caught in the crossfire and blamed for the downfall of the wizard Ponzi, the man who promised to make everyone rich.

Hart wasn't exactly a beautiful woman; she could be described more as handsome, and very elegant—a woman that could speak to paupers and kings and treat them all with the same kindness and dignity. It was that afternoon, as Hart lay on the couch trying to forget the difficult times, that the doorbell rang. She rose and opened the door to find two distinguished but extremely nervous looking women.

"Mrs. Allen," the taller of the two inquired, "may we come in, please? Perhaps you don't remember me, but we graduated together. I'm Mrs. Tucker, and this is my friend Mrs. Hughes. I must see your husband," said the fellow Smith College graduate. "It's of the gravest importance!" The look on her face mirrored her concern.

"Yes, I do remember you. Please come in and I'll ask if he is able to see you," Hart replied as she left the two standing in the foyer and went looking for Joe. She found him in the study.

"Joe, there's a woman here... a Mrs. Tucker."

He rose slowly from his desk and removed his glasses. "Hart, I don't want to see her. She is the wife of one of the officers of Hanover Bank who was arrested for mishandling bank funds. Tell her I'm ill and cannot see her."

Hart nodded and returned to give the women who were anxiously awaiting an answer. "I'm sorry, ladies, but Mr. Allen is not feeling well and cannot see you."

"Please, Mrs. Allen, convince your husband to see me. I have nowhere to turn. Please, I beg of you!" The woman was close to tears.

Hart returned to Joe and told him of the woman's insistence. Joe thought for a moment then finally gave in. "All right, I'll see her... but under no circumstances do you leave the room!" Hart and Joe entered the living room. Joe wore a robe, with his hair a bit disheveled purposely to appear ill.

"Mr. Allen, I'm Mrs. Robert Tucker. Is there anything in your power you can do to assist my husband in this horrible scandal?"

"I'm sorry, Mrs. Tucker, but the situation is completely out of my hands."

"There must be something you can do. After all, you're the bank commissioner. Please help him, for I'm very worried for his life." She began to sob. "He's become very despondent and I... I've noticed he has a gun in the house now."

Hart noticed Joe began to blanch, but he kept his ground. "Mrs. Tucker, believe me, there is nothing I can do. Tell your husband that he must hold on. Have faith. Truth will win out, I promise."

The woman dabbed her tear-filled eyes. "I hope you're right, sir," she said as she stood up, trying to compose herself. "Thank you for seeing me. Goodbye, Mrs. Allen."

"Goodbye," Hart answered as she showed the women to the door. She was so very proud of the way Joe had handled the situation. Even then, she sensed the great turmoil within him and the anguish and heartbreak that his discovery and actions had brought to so many others.

That dreadful year made her long for the safety of Chebegue and the wonderful memories connected with it. What was that story the mainlanders told? The Indians looked at the biggest island in Casco Bay and exclaimed, "She big." From that day forth the island was known as Chebegue. Every year the family spent the summer at Noddlehead, their home on Chebegue Island, which was just off the coast of Maine. Noddlehead was an enormous house covered with gray shingles. Tiny pink roses picked their way up the sides, clinging to each shingle and filling the air with their intoxicating scent. A large porch wound its way around the house, giving a sweeping view of the ocean as it licked the rocky shore. Perched on the edge of a craggy cliff, it was the perfect place to watch the sunset and, at night, listen to the rhythm of the waves as they pounded the shore. The building had a huge center fireplace where Hart read many a mystery on a stormy night, and a small ferry was the only access to and from the island. It was her favorite place, beginning when she was a little girl and continuing to the times she spent vacationing from Smith. Mother saw to it that they had fun things to do, and there was always a steady stream of visitors to keep them company, as well as many wonderful clambakes on the shore.

One of Hart's favorite pastimes was swimming across the bay and back. Mother disapproved of this, so Hart never told her of the time she became dizzy and barely made it back to shore, where she lay gasping on the beach trying to regain her strength. Mother and Father were wonderful to all the children. They always had their best interests at heart, even when Mother tried to pair her off with the neighbor's son Wesley. Mother thought he was the perfect match for Hart. She never forgot the day Mother told her he was coming to call. Hart was furious! She couldn't stand Wesley, and when mother announced his arrival, Hart ran out the back door, slid down the steep cliff, and hid at the water's edge. To this day she wondered how Mother explained her sudden disappearance!

Hart always waited with great anticipation for school to begin, and from the very first day she attended Smith College she loved it there. She had many friends and it was always great fun to bring them to the family home in Springfield, Massachusetts for the weekend. She always made sure the chauffeur took the roundabout way. Hart felt the area of the city surrounding "Apple Tree Corner" was not in keeping with the beauty of her home. She often felt pangs of guilt for seeming so snobbish, but Joseph understood. He would hold the car door open and with a secretive wink ask, "Take the long way home, Miss Harris?"

Hart would always answer with a smile, "Yes, Joseph. Let's show the girls Springfield."

She often came home on weekends. Hart loved spending time with the family, and since Smith was just a few miles away, Mother and Father indulged her. She would never forget that weekend in April of 1912 when she came home and found Mother very upset.

"What is it? What's wrong?"

Mother looked grave. "I have some very bad news." Her voice quavered. "The President of Yale called. Chesley hasn't been well. He's lost his appetite and has no energy. Father went to bring him home. The doctor will be here this afternoon." She sank into a chair. "I can't understand it, he was home for spring break and never said a word about feeling ill."

"Would it be better if I went back to Smith, Mother?"

"No, stay. You're a great comfort to me. Let's sit and have a cup of tea. Perhaps it will calm my nerves."

Hart sat with her mother and the two discussed the news of the ill-fated ship Titanic. "Wasn't our neighbor Milton Long aboard?" Hart asked.

"Yes, he was. I just hope luck was with him again this time. Joseph told me Milton gave his chauffeur his pocket watch before he left for the *Titanic*. I hope he wasn't having some sort of premonition..."

At that moment Joseph could be heard driving the Phaeton into the driveway. A few minutes later, Chesley entered the kitchen supported by Father, with Joseph close behind carrying the luggage. Hart was shocked at Chesley's gaunt and fragile appearance. She ran to him and hugged him tightly, trying to disguise her concern.

"I've missed you, Chess...why haven't you written?"

"I've missed you too, Hartie. I've been feeling so poorly, I haven't been up for any correspondence." Hart held her brother's hand and looked lovingly into his blue eyes. Chesley was twenty-three, and Hart three years younger, which gave them a special bond.

"Let me help you upstairs. Mother...have Cook make a cup of tea for Chess, will you?"

"Of course, dear. I'll bring it up." Mother kissed Chesley on the forehead. Hart and Chesley climbed the stairs arm in arm and walked to his bedroom. Inside, she helped him settle into bed.

"Chess, how long have you felt this way?"

"Oh, just a few weeks. Really, Hart, I'll be fine. I'll bounce right back, don't you worry." Chesley tried to maintain a positive outlook for her. Hart noticed Chess no longer had that sparkle in his eyes. He looked completely drained. Mother brought in the cup of tea and sat at the edge of the bed.

"Chesley, darling, why didn't you let us know you were ill?"

"...and worry the dickens out of you and Father? I'll be fine. I was just telling Hart I'll be as good as new in no time, now that I'm home and eating Mary Moriarty's cooking."

Mother smiled and brushed a stray lock of hair from Chesley's forehead. "And I'm going to hold you to that, young man," she answered sternly.

"Would you like me to turn the radio on for you?" asked Hart.

"Yes, that would be good, Hartie. I've been keeping track of the *Titanic* disaster. Isn't it terrible?"

"Yes. Did you know Judge Long's son Milton was a passenger? They are still waiting for confirmation of his being on the survivors list."

Hart interrupted, "Let's leave Chess to rest, Mother. Tell the maid to come get us when you feel like having some company, alright?"

"I will."

The two women slipped out of the room and Hart gently shut the door behind them. Hart turned to her mother and saw how greatly worried she had become.

"When is the doctor coming, Mother?"

"He should be here around four o'clock."

"Good, because I'm really afraid for Chess. He looks absolutely terrible. What could be wrong with him?"

"The physician at Yale suspects diabetes. He's been suffering from excessive thirst and he's lost considerable weight."

"Oh, no...I hope he's wrong."

Later that afternoon, the doctor came and gave Chesley a thorough examination. Their worst fears were realized when the doctor confirmed Hart's brother was suffering from acute diabetes. Hart went into Chesley's room shortly afterward.

"Did you hear the news, Hartie? Rotten luck, isn't it?"

"Oh, Chess, we are going to take good care of you. There will be no more of Mary Moriarty's desserts for you, dear brother." Hart tried to joke, but knew the situation was serious. Mother, Father, and Hart stood vigil all through the night. The doctor was called again at ten the next morning, when Chesley's condition began to deteriorate. The doctor did all he could, while the three waited in the study to hear the doctor's prognosis. Hart knew the news would be bad. It was not long before he walked in, placed his bag on the table, and muttered two words: "I'm sorry."

Mother grabbed the edge of the table to support herself. Father rushed over and put his arm around her.

The doctor sighed. "I'm afraid there is nothing we can do for Chesley. His diabetes is extremely advanced. I suspect he has had it for a year or more." Mother began to sob.

"But he's only twenty-three. He is to graduate in three weeks...this can't be," cried Hart.

"It's just a matter of time. All we can do is keep him comfortable." As the doctor left the room, Hart and her parents hugged each other and cried. The family and the entire household staff did everything they could to comfort Chesley in his final hours. The next afternoon, April 17, Chesley died in his bed at two o'clock, listening to the news of the *Titanic*.

Hart's graduation from Smith in 1913 was a much happier memory. Mother and Father were so proud, especially since Mother was an 1883 graduate of Smith as well. After graduation, Hart and her parents took a trip to the Orient. While in Japan, they were special guests of the Emperor in his breathtaking palace and garden. China, too, was mysterious and beautiful, and all she had imagined. It was on the return trip, aboard ship, that Hart met Bob Hutchins, a handsome man who swept her off her feet. She felt he was her soul mate. He was handsome and charming—exactly what a girl fresh out of college would find attractive. Hart was floating on a cloud when she returned to America with the promise she would write him faithfully still on her lips. Bob's letters were sizzling and romantic. He begged her to marry him, and said they would live in England, a condition necessitated by his advancing career with the British American Tobacco Company.

Mother and Father refused to allow Hart to announce an engagement because she would be forced to live abroad. They felt that Bob's interest stemmed from their financial position. She argued and argued with them, but finally agreed to wait. Not too long after, Hart received a curt letter from Bob calling their relationship off.

In the spring of 1918 Hart met Joseph Allen. Joe was twenty-two years older than she, a respectable gentleman with a fine position in a Springfield bank. They fell in love and decided to marry, choosing the week of Christmas for their wedding.

Hart awoke early that morning and thought, *December twenty-first! Finally the big day has arrived! It's my wedding day!*

She could hear all the bustling downstairs in the kitchen. Mary Moriarty had no doubt begun the final preparations for the evening. Mother could be heard giving last minute orders to everyone concerned. Hart sat in bed and gazed across the room at the lovely white gown lying on the chair. Mother had wanted Hart to wear her wedding gown, but there wasn't sufficient time for alterations, so she chose this lovely, simple white gown, topped off with an imported Italian lace collar her Aunt Rita had given her as a wedding gift.

The flu pandemic was raging in Springfield, with thousands of people dying throughout the country. Luckily, she and Joe had managed to avoid it. Hospitals had emergency quarters set up for the rising number of patients, some of which had to be placed in the halls. Due to the pandemic, the celebration was to include just the family and a few close friends. Mr. Seelye, president of Smith and an old friend of the family, was expected to officiate, and would arrive soon.

The Springfield house, a large, brick Victorian mansion, was humming with excitement. The large curved staircase, which had an eight-foot gilded mirror on each side, was festooned with flowers. All the rooms were decorated with flower arrangements, and the dining room was prepared for a banquet dinner. A lovely, small altar had been erected in the living room for the service.

Evening came quickly and Hart began to prepare for the ceremony. She was so proud that she was soon to become Mrs. Joseph Allen. Joe had begun his career as a mere messenger at the Second National Bank, and through dedication and an uncanny knowledge of banking worked his way up to treasurer of the Hampden Trust Bank. There was talk of consolidation between Hampden and Union Trust and the possibility of Joe being promoted to vice president. Hart had indeed made a wise choice for a husband.

Hart's sister Ambia burst into the room and breathlessly announced, "The ceremony is about to begin, Hartie! Are you ready?"

"Yes, Bobby...tell Mother I'm ready," said Hart, smiling as she turned and stole a last glance at herself in the mirror. The distant strains of the "Wedding March" drifted up to her room. She descended the staircase and joined Father, who awaited her at the bottom. Hart took his arm and together they slowly walked to the living room.

"You look lovely, Hart," Father whispered.

"Oh, Father, this is the happiest day of my life."

Hart and Joe's eyes met. As President Seelye began the vows, she gave her hand to Joe and became oblivious to everyone else present.

Immediately after the ceremony, the family escorted the couple to the train station. The train ride to Hartford was exciting. Hart sat next to the window with Joe at her side. The car was filled with young soldiers on leave for the holidays, and spirits were so high everyone was singing. The soldiers must have guessed they were newlyweds, as they kept jumping up and saluting the happy couple.

"Do you think we will always be this happy, Joe?"

"I know we will, Hart, we have each other," was his loving reply.

Hart rested her head on the back of the seat and closed her eyes, listening to the sound of the train wheels. They would be spending the night in Hartford and in the morning continue on their honeymoon trip to Virginia, after which they would return to Springfield and go about starting their promising life together.

Chapter 2

Charles Ponzi spent a depressing day in his cold-water flat in Somerville, Massachusetts, with his beautiful wife, Rose. Ponzi was born in Lugo, Italy, in 1882, and came to America with one burning desire: to become rich!

"You deserve more than this, Rose," Ponzi said as he shook his head sadly. "I've tried everything, but I've failed you."

"Charlie, you know I love you very much, and nothing else matters. You don't have to buy me jewels; your love is all that I want and need. Can't you see how happy you make me?"

She whirled around smiling and kissed her husband on the forehead. Rose Gnecco, the twenty-year-old daughter of a fruit peddler, had the face of an angel, with delicate features and shining eyes. Her dark, curly hair danced around her face before it cascaded down to her milk white shoulders. Her lush body belied her tender age, and her laugh could be seductive or childlike, making her the most captivating creature the thirty-seven year old Ponzi had ever met. Right from their first meeting he was dazzled by her beauty, and he truly adored her.

"Rose, just wait. Someday you'll see. You will dress like a queen with jewels and furs, and you will live in a mansion and ride in a big, beautiful car, I promise you!" Rose laughed and turned her attention to preparing the pasta.

There must be a way to become rich. I must think up a plan of some sort, he thought as he scanned the newspaper.

Ponzi had already exhausted several avenues—working as a fruit peddler, waiting on tables, and working as a clerk—since his arrival in the "Promised Land." However, through it all, Ponzi felt he was destined to become an influential man with unlimited finances.

"Oh, Charlie, I almost forgot, you got a letter from Spain. It's on the *tavola*," Rose announced excitedly, bringing his thoughts back to the present. Charlie opened the letter and found it was from a company he had done importing business with in the past. Enclosed along with the letter was an International Reply Coupon.

"*Mangia*, Charlie," Rose called as she began to set the table.

"After lunch I am going to the post office, Rose. I want to find out more about this coupon," said Ponzi as he looked it over curiously.

Later that afternoon he walked through the post office, his footsteps echoing on the marble floor. He stepped up to a window, removed his hat, and gave a slight cough to capture the attention of the postal clerk.

"Pardon me please, could you tell me what this reply coupon is?"

"Sure, buddy, it works like this: If you send a letter from Spain to the United States, you can buy a reply coupon for one cent, and it can be used as a six cent stamp here."

"Aha, I see," Ponzi answered. "One cent in another country and six cents here, hmm, that's very interesting," he thought, stroking his chin. Walking home, Ponzi kept thinking of the coupons, and the more he thought, the more excited he became.

He rushed to Luigi Casullo's store and stepped inside. To Ponzi's relief, as he quickly glanced around he noticed that the store was empty of customers. His mind raced at the possibilities. If he could buy one stamp in Spain for one cent and cash it in for six cents in the United States because the money exchange was higher, why couldn't he buy hundreds, thousands, millions of these coupons? He would give the ordinary person a chance to invest with him, and perhaps offer them a higher rate of interest than they receive from the bank. He could then use that money to buy up more coupons. It could be a huge business. He could hire employees and maybe later open several offices. *It could be a money machine, a powerful engine making me and many others very rich. This could be it; this could be the great plan I've dreamed about*, he thought excitedly.

"I need two hundred dollars, could you loan it to me? It's very important!"

Luigi looked up from the counter. "Whatza matter? Is Rosa sick?"

"No, no, Rose is fine," Ponzi answered. "I need the money for something else. I'll pay you fifty percent interest in forty-five days, I promise you," he replied, shaking with excitement.

"Charlie, two hundred dollars is a lotta money, but...for a friend, I guess it'sa alright."

The two friends went to the back room, where Luigi counted out the money. Charlie quickly scooped it up, and as he stuffed it into his pocket he explained his plan to Luigi.

"I know it will work, my *compare*..."

"But how will-a you tell the people, Charlie?" Luigi asked with a puzzled look.

"We'll tell everyone right away. We'll spread the word. You can help. Tell all your customers I will help them to get rich. I'll let you know where my office will be and you just send them there. *Capisce*?" Charlie's excitement had built to a fever pitch.

"How much interest did you say?" Luigi asked wrinkling his fat, mustached face.

"Fifty percent in forty-five days and 100 percent in ninety days...better than any bank, Luigi. And we will take any amount, no matter how small. I want everyone to have a chance to make some money! I'm never going to forget this, Luigi. This is going to make us both rich," Ponzi yelled over his shoulder as he hurried for the door.

Luigi just shook his head and chuckled. "That'sa Charlie...he'sa always gotta some big idea!"

That evening, Rose carefully folded Charlie's suit pants, hung them on a hanger, and placed them in the closet. Lifting the jacket and giving it a quick brushing, she placed it, too, on a hanger, and was about to hang it up when she noticed a large bulge in the pocket. To her amazement, Rose reached in and dug out a fistful of twenty-dollar bills!

"Charlie, come here."

"What is it, Rose? What's the matter?" Charlie asked innocently. Rose held out the wad of bills. "This money, Charlie, where did you get it?"

"I borrowed it from Luigi. I was going to tell you about it later, Rose."

"What are you going to do with it, Charlie?"

"Don't worry about it...let's go to bed." His eyes glistened as his hand slipped around her waist, and he pulled her to him.

The next morning, Ponzi rose early and began his hunt for an office. The plan was to start his operation and gradually expand as word of mouth spread. After much searching, he chose the Bell-In-Hand Tavern in William Court (also known as Pie Alley, a relic of the Revolutionary days) in the heart of Boston's financial district.

On the following day, he asked the young man next door if he would like a part time job. Tom Martini readily accepted, and together they walked to the office. Tom carried some crates up the stairs to the second floor room and noticed that it was quite stuffy. Ponzi busied himself arranging the meager pieces of furniture.

"Tom, help me turn over this crate. We'll use it for a desk."

"Yes, Mr. Ponzi." *I guess it'll do for now*, Tom thought.

A sound in the doorway made both men look up with a start. There stood a man with his cap in his hands.

"*Bon giorno*, Ponzi. I hav'a some money to give'a you. Twenty dollars, si?"

"*Bon giorno*, Tony. It's good to see you. Come in, come in!" Ponzi shook the man's hand. "How did you hear about my business, Tony?"

"Luigi told me. He says you promise'a fifty percent interest on'a my money in'a forty-five days. Is'a that right?"

"That's right, Tony, and one hundred per cent in ninety days."

"Well, you keep'a my money for forty-five days. If'a you keep'a your promise, Charlie, I will give'a you some more money. It'sa deal?"

"It's a deal, Tony." Ponzi smiled as he quickly scribbled out a receipt and handed it to his first client.

The day passed quickly. Ponzi was quite satisfied with the number of people that had visited his office. Scratching his head, he whispered, "Twenty-three people have visited my office today. Judging from the amount of receipts, my first day in business was very successful." His smile grew even broader when he glanced at the shoebox full of money.

"Not bad for a day's work, not bad at all! Tom, let's close up. Make a sign that reads 'Open at 9:00' and hang it up on your way out."

"You bet, Mr. Ponzi," Tom answered with admiration in his voice. He was amazed at the amount of money he and his boss had collected.

"What are you going to do with all the money, sir?"

"I'll deposit it in the bank on my way home. Here's two dollars, buy something for your mother. Don't forget to tell her all about my new business, and tell her to tell all her friends!"

"I sure will! See you tomorrow morning."

The young man ran downstairs and a few moments later could be heard nailing up the sign. Ponzi looked around the crude office and reflected. "This is a good beginning, but only a beginning. Soon the name Charles Ponzi will be on everyone's lips."

He deposited the day's collection in the Hanover Bank on his way home, all except for a small amount he kept to purchase Rose some gifts. He stopped at Rossi's Fruit Market and bought some oranges, apples, and bananas. Up until now, Charlie hadn't been able to afford to buy his loving wife fresh fruit with his meager earnings. He mentioned his business to the peddler, thinking that a little advertising wouldn't hurt.

He climbed the stairs to his flat on the third floor, whistling softly. *This will change*, he thought. *I'll buy a beautiful home, nothing but the best for us!*

Juggling the bags, he took out his key and let himself into the apartment.

"Rose, I'm home!"

Rose came into the kitchen and stared in amazement at the bags spilling over the kitchen table.

"Charlie, fresh fruit...how wonderful!" They hugged and Ponzi withdrew a small bag from inside his jacket. Rose took it and peeked inside.

"Candy sticks and peppermints!" she exclaimed. The couple kissed and held each other tightly for several moments.

"Rose, my first day in business was wonderful! Tom Martini and I collected over 200 dollars. If it continues like this, I will have to hire another clerk! Tomorrow I will go to City Hall and register my business. I'm going to call it the Security Exchange Company."

"But Charlie, what kind of business is it?"

"Don't worry your pretty little head about it. Just leave all the thinking to me. From now on we are going to live!"

That night, lying in bed, he considered all the necessary changes he would have to make in the office. *If I continue to collect great amounts of money I had better improve security,* he thought. *I'll have to set up some type of grill for protection so that I don't have to worry about a stick-up.*

Business was tremendous the next day. A line of people had formed on the stairs leading to the office. Ponzi's offer was the talk of the streets, and everyone was curious. The office was crudely furnished, but that did nothing to detract from the impeccably dressed Ponzi. He sat behind his orange crate dressed in a suit with a flower in his lapel, his straw hat perched on the makeshift desk. His eyes twinkled with delight as some neighbors and some strangers entered the room single file. *Perhaps doctors, lawyers, politicians, policemen, and maybe even a banker or two will buy a part of my business,* he thought. *Now wouldn't that be a kick in the pants,* he chuckled. Two women slowly approached Ponzi's desk.

"Mrs. Bartoni, Mrs. Rossi, buon giorno!" gushed the silver-tongued charmer as he stood and gave a deep bow. He pulled a handkerchief from his breast pocket with a flourish and dusted off his chair. Arranging the papers on his desk, he flashed his ever-present million-dollar smile.

"Hello, Charlie. We want to buy a piece of'a your business," one of the women announced.

"Wonderful! You won't be sorry...I promise you that!"

"Ah...Charlie, whatever you do, don't tell Dominic. I'm using the money from my sugar bowl." She winked at him. "How you say, a nest egg? I want to surprise him. It'sa alright?"

"That's fine, Mrs. Rossi, I won't say a word." Ponzi turned to his young clerk. "Here, Tom, give Mrs. Rossi a receipt for twenty dollars."

"Mr. Rossi was in here earlier this morning, Mr. Ponzi," Tom told his boss in a low whisper.

"Thank you, thank you! You are two very smart ladies," Ponzi went on, ignoring the young man's remark.

In the next few weeks, the number of transactions grew, making it almost impossible for the two to handle the crowds.

"If this is a sample of things to come, I'll be a millionaire in no time," Ponzi reasoned to himself.

The news of fast-earned money was spreading quickly, and Charlie noticed many of the people that were coming to invest were strangers to him. It was time to find another location, he thought, perhaps one a little closer to the center of the city where he could attract people of influence and affluence. The larger quarters, located at 27 School Street, was an eleven-by-thirty-six-foot room divided into three compartments with crude partitions. Charlie hired four new clerks to handle the increase in business.

He sat at a flattop desk with a newly hired secretary opposite him. The door had a patented lock, which could only be opened from the inside, and a button on Ponzi's desk opened and closed the lock. Clients paid their money through three roughly-made iron grills. The room was thick with cigarette smoke, with Charlie's ever-present cigar adding to the haze. It reminded him of one of the Italian bordellos he visited when he was a young man. It was stiflingly hot as the clerks, with shirtsleeves rolled up and perspiration dripping off their brows, raked in the money. After quickly writing off receipts, they shoveled piles of money off the rough wooden floor into laundry baskets lined up at the back wall. There was money everywhere, a truly incredible sight to behold. Later that day all baskets would be removed from the building and delivered to the bank to be deposited in Ponzi's account. Out of the dirty window Ponzi watched as crowds of people formed a long, twisting line down the middle of the street, like a huge, thick snake, often stopping traffic. A policeman directed the vehicles around the line of investors, shaking his head in amazement. It was a circus atmosphere as people talked excitedly of how they were using their life savings to get rich quick. Some boasted of re-mortgaging their home, cashing their insurance policies, and even selling their automobiles just so they could take a chance on a dream with the "wizard of odds!"

Chapter 3

The streets of Boston were dark and deserted as the black sedan came to a stop, parking at the edge of the dock. The waves slapped against the pier and the moon shone down on the rippling water. Two men exited the vehicle, walked to the back, and lifted the trunk lid. Struggling to lift a body from the trunk, one whispered to the other.

"Grab his feet, Rocky, the bastard weighs a ton! He's a goddamn elephant! Put him down for a minute, will ya?"

The two men laid the body down on the ground, and Marco lit a cigarette. Pulling up his collar, he inhaled deeply and blew a puff of smoke into the cool night air.

"I think it's gonna rain. I can smell it!"

"For Chrissakes," Rocky barked, "who asked ya for a weather report? Let's dump this load into the river and get the hell out of here!"

The two men carried the large form to the edge of the dock, rolled it into the water, and watched it silently disappear.

"How deep is the water here, anyway?" Marco asked, his face wrinkled with curiosity.

"Why? You plannin' to take a swim?" Rocky answered sarcastically.

Marco threw his cigarette into the water. "Haha...very funny!"

Watching the cigarette disappear, Rocky answered, "Don't worry, it's plenty deep. With that rock he's carrying in his lap, he's goin' nowhere but to the bottom."

Marco rubbed his hands together. "Hey, let's get somethin' to eat, I'm starvin'."

Rocky agreed. "Good idea!"

The two men walked back to the car. Rocky slammed the trunk closed and they both climbed into the vehicle. They swiftly traveled through the waterfront area and stopped at Sharkey's. Yes, Sharkey's was *the* place in town. It was on a side street in Boston, yet known to all the wise guys and their dames. Difficult to describe—you could call it a bar, a restaurant, a club—but most importantly you would call it "unique." A long bar occupied one whole side of the establishment with the usual stools, while the opposite side featured several booths. The center of the room was filled with tables and chairs, but the prominent attraction was a huge aquatic tank displaying a live blue shark. Appropriate? Yes! A tongue and cheek whim, cooked up by the many "loan sharks" that frequented the place. Exiting the car and quickly looking around, the two entered the back door.

Sauntering through the kitchen, Marco yelled, "Gino, two plates of pasta. No...make that two bowls of *Pasta fagiole.*"

"You bet, boys...right away," came the quick reply.

The two men found a booth and slid in. Soon Gino delivered the soup, along with a loaf of bread and a bottle of wine. The two began to eat ravenously.

Stuffing his mouth with bread, Marco remarked, "This is great! So...why do you think we had to whack that guy?"

"Don't know. We just do what we're told, right?" Rocky answered between slurps.

Marco jabbed his finger in the air to make a point. "I think the bastard crossed the boss, which made him not long for this world!"

Rocky laughed, "You ain't shittin' there!"

"Hey, you goin' over to your broad's house tonight?" Marco asked, wiping his mouth on his sleeve.

"Nah, I think I'll go home. Helen is tryin' to rent out the second floor apartment in her house, and she said she's got to show it early tomorrow morning."

Marco laughed. "Oh, yah, and everybody knows how she loves 'showin' it!" Rocky reached across the table and grabbed Marco's shirt.

"Cut the shit, or I'll break your rotten neck!"

"Okay, okay, just kiddin'. Jesus Christ, relax," Marco nervously pleaded as he straightened his shirt.

Agitated, Rocky stood up to leave. "Come on, pay the bill and let's go."

Outside, Marco got into the driver's seat and looked over at Rocky.

"How about stoppin' at the Ice House and seein' if we can scare up a couple of guys for a card game?"

"That's the best idea you had all day!" Rocky answered in a better mood. After a short ride the two arrived at the Ice House, a large brick building with a steel door and a dock attached to the front. The lot in front of the building was full, so after parking the car in the back, they got out and walked around to the front door.

"Well, it should be no problem gettin' a game goin'; looks like a full house tonight. Wonder what's goin' on?" Marco remarked under his breath.

They walked in the front door and looked around. Several men were busy working around the ice pits.

Rocky asked three men working a pit, "What the hell's goin' on here?"

"Ya know that punk on the West Side...the one that's been givin' you guys all that shit?" one asked.

Rocky nodded, "Yah, what about 'em?"

"He's chillin' out," grinned the iceman.

He gestured to the pit and Rocky and Marco peered in. A huge block of ice was floating below with a man suspended inside, a look of agony and horror on his frozen, colorless face. Marco rolled his eyes, his cigarette dangling from his lips.

"Jesus...doesn't this place make little ice cubes anymore?" he asked nonchalantly.

Amused, the iceman answered, "Yah, sometimes ...but whatever we 'make,' boys, always comes outta here cold and stiff."

Everyone laughed as the men attached a rope to the overhead pulley and lifted the frozen form out of the pit.

Chapter 4

Hart and Joe arrived at the Springfield Depot at 4:30. Collecting their baggage, they hurried out to the street, fighting the crowd of commuters.

"Does Mother Allen know when to send the chauffeur, Joe?"

"I called her and told her we should arrive here at about 4:30. I don't think we'll have to wait too long, Hart."

Thank goodness, thought Hart, as she shifted her weight from one foot to the other. "My feet are killing me!"

Her thoughts slipped back to Virginia and their wonderful honeymoon. She began to giggle, and Joe looked at her questioningly.

"I was just thinking about the ride on the ferry, when we were walking on deck and the wind blew your glasses into the ocean!"

Joe's face slowly broke into a grin. She stole a side-glance at Joe just as he glanced at her, and they both began to laugh. At that moment the Allen car pulled up. The familiar face of John, the family chauffeur, was a welcome sight. He quickly stepped out of the car and opened the back door for the newlyweds.

"Enjoy your trip, Sir?"

"Splendid...just not long enough."

"How are Mother and Father Allen?" inquired Hart.

"They are just fine, Madam. The family is anxiously awaiting your arrival!" The ride to the Allen house was short. The old mansion was ablaze with lights. Hart noticed someone peering through the living room window as they climbed from the car. The huge door swung open and Maggie, the maid, stood in the foyer, her face beaming.

"Welcome home, Mr. and Mrs. Allen. We're so happy to have you back!" boomed the heavyset woman. Maggie had the face of a leprechaun and an Irish brogue as thick as Mulligan's Stew.

"Thank you, Maggie. It's wonderful to be home!" answered Joe. "Where are Mother and Father?"

"They are upstairs dressing for dinner, Sir. Georgianna and Alice are in the living room."

Joe's two sisters excitedly rushed in. Alice couldn't keep her enthusiasm in check. "Joe, Hart, welcome home!" She gave them both a big hug.

John stacked the luggage in the foyer as Joe handed the coats and hats to Maggie. The two sisters quickly guided the couple into the living room.

"Sit near the fireplace while I pour you both a well-deserved sherry," ordered Georgie.

Hart and Joe smiled at each other as Georgie poured the liquor and served it to them on a silver tray. Hart sipped the drink and enjoyed the warm feeling it gave her.

"Tell me," bubbled Alice, "did you have a nice trip?"

Joe and Hart described some of the events, ending with the story of the ferryboat ride. Georgie and Alice laughed at the prospect of their big brother getting into such a situation. Soon Mother and Father Allen entered the room.

"My dears, how delightful to have you back," exclaimed Mother Allen. "Hart...you look wonderful!" She crossed the room and embraced her new daughter-in-law.

"You look to be in good health, Mother Allen. I presume the Allen family was able to sidestep the flu?"

"We certainly were fortunate, indeed. I suspect you both must be quite exhausted from the trip. Would you like to go upstairs and rest until dinner?"

"Yes, I think that is an excellent idea," Father Allen added. "There will be plenty of time to talk later."

Hart and Joe climbed the stairs to the upstairs chambers with the maid leading the way. Hart could feel the effects of the trip and was thankful for the suggestion of a short rest.

Later, at dinner, the entire family sat around the dining room table and feasted on the sumptuous meal. The Allen's cook had outdone herself as usual, with a deliciously roasted chicken and a host of side dishes. Everyone enjoyed the meal and an air of celebration filled the evening.

"Mother Allen, did I ever tell you of my first attempt at making chicken soup?" asked Hart.

"No, I don't believe you have, Hart."

"Well, my sister Bobby and I were at Noddlehead in Maine, and Mother and Father were at home in Springfield. There was a good deal of flu on the island, so we sent word to them not to come up, as we were concerned about their health; besides, Bobby and I felt we could get along nicely by ourselves. Every week we would have a visit from the cobbler, who would pick up the family shoes, repair them, and leave them wrapped on the porch. We also had a bread man and a poultry man that made regular deliveries. Mother was fond of fresh chickens, and had one delivered to Noddlehead quite often. I saw to it that the packages were put on ice, and tried to keep the household running as smoothly as possible. Meanwhile, Bobby came down with an absolutely miserable case of the flu."

"Oh my, what ever did you do?" asked Mother Allen.

"Well, I offered to make her some chicken soup, and Bobby was delighted! I put a large kettle of water on the stove and removed one of the packages from the icebox. I opened it, and to my surprise inside was a pair of shoes. In fact, all the packages on ice were shoes; there were no chickens. I laughed so hard, but Bobby was so upset she cried. She had been all prepared for hot chicken soup!"

"Oh, dear," Alice said with a chuckle, "I think the first thing you had better do, Joe, is hire a cook!" With that, everyone laughed, including Hart.

Joe and Hart began the move to Aunt Rita's apartment the following morning, where they would live until they were able to find a place of their own. Aunt Rita was abroad and wasn't expected back for some time.

The newlyweds moved in, and within weeks Joe's career began to take off. He was named Vice President of Union Trust Bank. One afternoon, a few weeks later, Joe came home from the bank and burst into the living room with more exciting news.

"Hart, you will never guess who will be visiting Springfield next month."

Hart looked up from her sewing. "Who, Joe, who?"

"Enrico Caruso!"

"Oh, that's wonderful! How did you find out about it?"

"A local club is bringing him in for a private concert, and I have been asked to make the arrangements!" he proudly announced.

Hart was astonished. "Does that mean that we will be able to attend?"

"Absolutely!"

"Joe, this is so exciting! Where will he perform? How many are expected to attend?" She suddenly looked anxious. "What ever shall I wear?"

"Slow down, Hart...one question at a time!"

"Oh, you know how I love his singing. I can't wait to meet him!"

The weeks passed slowly as Hart prepared for the important event. On the day of Caruso's concert, Hart piled her long hair on top of her head in a beautiful up-sweep. She had purchased a lovely gown of teal blue and a matching pair of shoes, and was looking forward to the evening with great anticipation. While sitting at the vanity and buffing her nails she heard Joe let himself into the apartment.

"Hartie?"

"I'm in the bedroom getting ready, Joe."

"I have a surprise for you!"

Hart rushed over to him. "Oh, let me see what you're holding behind you!" Joe brought his hand out and presented her with an orchid corsage.

"How beautiful!"

"Are you ready for an exciting evening? You know, we're very fortunate to be in the company of the great Caruso!"

"We certainly are! It's quite an honor...and to have dinner with him, that will be the icing on the cake!"

That evening, looking around the table, Hart privately assessed the other guests. The bank president and his wife were a lovely couple, and it was easy to see they were in awe of the great tenor. To Hart's left sat the president of the club, who had enlisted Caruso for this private concert. Across from her sat her distinguished-looking husband, quite a bit older than his wife, Hart noticed. Joe sat across from Hart, and to her right, at the head of the table, sat the hostess of the dinner party. The woman had managed to titter away a great part of the evening, much to the discomfort of all those present. Whether due to nervousness, or perhaps a lack of good breeding, she made a complete spectacle of herself, and appeared to embarrass Caruso as she constantly fished for compliments.

Later, Caruso announced to all present that he enjoyed drawing as a hobby and would like to draw a caricature of each guest on their dinner napkin, which they could keep as a souvenir. Everyone was delighted with the idea. Each guest posed as the Great Caruso quickly drew a sketch of them and signed his famous name beneath. Both Hart and Joe were quite satisfied with his rendition of the two of them.

As the evening drew to a close, Caruso stood and thanked everyone for making his trip to America an interesting and happy one. When asked of his future plans, he stated that he would continue to sing as long as he could, and that he wished that he would die before he lost his voice. Singing was what he enjoyed most in life, and without it there was nothing! Hart had the caricatures framed and proudly displayed them on the living room wall. Soon, much to Hart's sadness, a falling prop struck Caruso while on stage. Hart would always remember that wonderful night, and when Caruso passed away Hart donated the dinner napkins with their caricatures to the Springfield Museum for all to see and enjoy.

Chapter 5

Rose woke early and noticed Charlie hadn't left for the office yet. She leaned over and kissed him, brushing away a lock of hair from his forehead. "Charlie," she whispered so as not to startle him, "you're going to be late for work."

"Charlie?"

Suddenly, Charlie grabbed her and together they rolled across the bed. He kissed her and looked into her dark eyes.

"I love you, Rose. You're the best thing that ever happened to me."

"I love you too, Charlie."

She saw the familiar look in his eyes, and she knew he wanted her as much as she wanted him. His kisses were demanding and soon they were making love. Later, Rose felt the sunlight as it streaked through the window and fell across her body. She was content knowing she had Charlie to love and take care of her.

"Are you taking the day off?"

"Yes, we have something very important to do today. You and I are taking a ride—I have something to show you."

Rose dressed quickly, wondering what he had planned for them. After breakfast they went downstairs and ordered a cab. When the cab arrived, they climbed in and Ponzi gave an unfamiliar address to the driver.

A brief ride took them across town, and Rose peered out the window trying to recognize the area. They stepped out, Charlie taking Rose's hand.

"Where are we going?" she questioned.

Ponzi smiled broadly. "Right in here, where you will choose our first car!"

"Oh, do you mean it?"

"Come on, let's go," Charlie said, laughing as he tugged her by the arm to the door. Inside she gazed around at some of the most beautiful automobiles she had ever seen.

"These are not for us, Charlie."

"Come follow me and I'll show you the one that I like," Charlie declared excitedly, ignoring her remark. He led her to another display room and pointed.

"There it is, over there!"

Rose followed Charlie's finger and drew in her breath. There, in the corner, stood an enormous cream-colored limousine with salmon-colored silk upholstery.

"My God, Charlie, it's beautiful!"

A salesman joined the couple and asked if he could be of service, a look of doubt on his face. Charlie smiled and withdrew several hundred dollars from his wallet.

"We'd like to buy that automobile. Will this do as a down payment?" Ponzi asked the totally surprised man, who nodded and graciously opened the car door.

"I'll be back tomorrow with the balance," the Italian added in a casual manner.

Charlie leaned over and whispered to his wife, "Notice how his attitude has changed? Now we are being treated royally. It just proves the old saying, 'Money talks.'"

The couple climbed in and Rose leaned back and felt her body sink into the plush upholstery. She closed her eyes and smiled. "This feels wonderful."

Charlie's mind slipped back to the past, when owning his own automobile was only a dream. He used public transportation or relied on his own two feet. He often found it necessary to plug the holes in his shoes with pieces of cardboard to protect them from the rain and snow. Each night he would paint his shoes with black stove-polish, as well as apply a dab here and there on the worn parts of his black suit. But now...well, now he was living the "good life."

"Come on, Rose, let's have some lunch and then I'll show you the other surprise."

The couple walked to a quaint little restaurant across the street. After they were seated, Charlie began to tell her of his newfound success.

"Business has developed beyond my wildest dreams. Everyone is talking about my Security Exchange Company. In February I collected $5,800, and so far this month the total turned in is $28,724! Before too long I'll even have the politicians in City Hall eating out of my hands." His voice lowered. "I have great plans, Rose. I want to eventually organize my own chain of banks throughout the world. Perhaps I'll establish a large import/export business to operate steamship lines between Boston and foreign countries. All the profits will revert back to the stockholders in the form of dividends! People will be clamoring to invest with such assured profits."

"You sound like such a different person when you talk about this company," Rose said, shaking her head in disbelief.

"It's because I know this idea of mine will work. In fact, it has already begun to work. Business has increased a hundred-fold. Rose, I have had to hire five more agents to handle the number of customers waiting outside the office each day! Tomorrow I'll hire a chauffeur and have him bring you down to see for yourself," he promised.

After a leisurely lunch, the couple left the restaurant and hailed another cab. They rode down a quiet and beautiful tree-lined street. On each side stood elegant mansions with neatly clipped hedges and wide front lawns. The vehicle slowly turned into a driveway and stopped under a large portico. The house was a palatial residence in historic Lexington, with a veranda running around the second floor and atop the portico.

There were many large windows, most of which were topped with huge, striped awnings. Ponzi paid the cab driver and the couple got out and looked at the impressive structure. Ponzi started for the front door. "Let's go ring the bell and see who's home."

Rose turned white and pulled him back. "Oh my God, Charlie! You can't do that. We don't want to disturb anyone!"

"It's all right, Rose, we are to be given a tour of the place by a realtor."

"Do you mean you are planning to BUY this house?"

"Of course, if it's to our liking," he answered facetiously, a wide grin on his face.

The doorbell sounded and almost instantly an elderly man opened the door.

"Come in, Mr. and Mrs. Ponzi, you're right on time. I'm Mr. Davis."

Rose stepped into the foyer, wide-eyed, as he shook Charlie's hand.

"As you can see, this lovely home is ready for immediate occupancy. The floor in this entryway, along with the entire foyer, is covered with Italian marble."

Their footsteps echoed as the three moved into the large hall. Rose gazed in awe at the curved staircase leading up to the second floor.

"The room to the right is the dining room. It has a black marble fireplace, walnut paneling, and lovely casement windows," continued the realtor as they entered the huge room. "This dining room is large enough to seat thirty people, so hopefully you enjoy doing a good deal of entertaining. That chandelier, by the way, is made of imported crystal!" Mr. Davis pointed out.

"Oh, yes," Ponzi answered as he smiled at Rose and gave her a secretive wink. The three proceeded out across the hall and through a pair of ornately carved doors.

"This is the library. It also has walnut paneling, and, as you can see, numerous book cases as well. The fireplace on the far wall is made of Italian marble, and the French doors lead out onto the terrace."

Rose's head was spinning from the luxury of it all, and she grabbed Charlie's hand to help steady herself.

"This door leads to the back of the house," continued Mr. Davis. "Here we have an excellent kitchen with all the newest conveniences, and adjoining it is a nice butler's pantry." Mr. Davis pushed open a swinging door to reveal a room lined with many shelves and its own small sink. Ponzi noticed a narrow staircase in one corner of the kitchen.

"Where does that lead?" he asked.

"That, Sir, is the back staircase used by the help. It leads to the third floor where the maid's quarters are located."

Charlie thought of the many back staircases he had climbed when he worked as a gardener, and again as a butler, always trying to remain invisible, yet being there for every beck and call of the master and mistress of the house.

Mr. Davis interrupted Charlie's thoughts. "We, however, will take the main staircase, so that I may show you the bedrooms on the second floor."

The three returned to the front hall and began their ascent. Rose stopped briefly and turned to take a peek at the foyer from the top of the stairs. It was more beautiful than before. She hurried to join the two men as they entered a large room to the right of the staircase.

"This is the master bedroom. It's spacious and bright, plus it has generous closet space and an adjoining bathroom."

Rose gazed around at the beautiful, mauve room, thinking what a far cry it was from the tiny bedroom she and Charlie now shared.

"There are three more bedrooms and two and a half baths," declared the salesman.

Two and a half baths...all in the house and not out in the hall, Charlie thought, *what luxury!*

"Surely, a home anyone would be proud to own," Mr. Davis assured the couple.

"Indeed it is," agreed Ponzi. "I think it is exactly what we're looking for." He turned to his wife. "What do you think, Rose?"

"I...I...I think it's beautiful, Charlie," she stammered.

"Exactly what business are you in, Mr. Ponzi?" asked the realtor, excited over a prospective sale.

"I'm...er...in investments. I have an office in Boston, and I plan to open a branch office here in Lexington, soon!"

"Wonderful," Mr. Davis said, rubbing his hands together. "I think you and this house are well suited for each other!"

"Yes, you are quite right." Ponzi scanned the lower floor from the top of the stairs. *This house will help realize another small part of my dream,* he thought. *Tiny flats with shared bathrooms, and rats (the four legged kind) for neighbors will be a thing of the past.* "Have your office make up the necessary papers and deliver them to my office," Ponzi announced, extending his business card.

"It will be my pleasure, Sir." The two men shook hands to close the deal.

Chapter 6

Hart and Joe wanted a child more than anything else in the world—so much so that when they heard of the desperate situation the neighbor's maid was in, they immediately decided she might be the answer to their prayers. One afternoon, while waiting for the girl to visit, Joe straightened his tie and nervously looked at Hart.

"I hope you've got the story straight, and that the girl is being honest with you, Hart."

"She can hardly be anything else, Joe. I'm sure she is very frightened and confused. After all, she is only sixteen years old. I can imagine how a young girl discovering she is pregnant could conjure up all sorts of horrors."

The doorbell signaled Catherine's arrival.

"Let me take your coat, dear," Hart said softly. She led the girl into the living room and introduced her to Joe.

"Catherine, this is my husband, Joe. Joe, this is Amelia's maid, Catherine. How are you feeling?"

"I've been just fine. I paid the doctor bill with the money you gave me."

"That's good, dear. If there is anything else you need money for please let us know, won't you?"

"Thank you, yes I will."

"I have arranged for you to check into a clinic next month. They will monitor your condition and give you the best of care. Mr. Allen and I will pay all the expenses."

"You've been so kind to me," Catherine said, wiping tears from her eyes. "I don't know what I would have done without your offer of help," she cried.

"Now, now, don't upset yourself. Everything will turn out just fine."

"When Danny promised to marry me, I thought all my dreams were coming true. I would stay in America and we could start our own little family. I never thought he would just disappear and leave me all alone."

"I don't want you to feel you're alone, Catherine. We will be there with you, and you can be sure that we will love your child as though it were our own. It will have everything it needs, including the finest education available."

Catherine clumsily rose. "Thank you so much, I know I can count on you to do the best for my baby."

Hart and Joe stood and followed the girl to the door.

"Stop by next week and we'll make the final arrangements for your hospitalization. And please dear, don't worry about a thing."

Joe helped Catherine put on her coat, after which she turned and smiled. "I won't, Mr. and Mrs. Allen." She quickly let herself out the door.

Time rushed by and before they knew it the date for Catherine's admittance to the hospital had arrived. The antiseptic smell filled her nostrils as Hart walked down the hall, quickly reading the room numbers and anxiously searching for Room 312. It was located at the end of the corridor. Hart found Catherine lying in bed looking sadly out the window. *She looks like a child herself*, Hart thought.

"Catherine, I came as soon as I could."

The young girl turned her head and tears began to roll down her cheeks.

"Mrs. Allen, I'm so frightened. This is my first time away from my family and I feel so alone." Catherine's brogue was becoming quite thick. Hart noticed it always did when the girl became excited.

"Now, now, please don't upset yourself. It's bad for you and the baby." Hart was careful not to say *your baby*. "I think it would be an excellent idea for us to hire a private nurse for you. This way you'll always have someone with you."

A nurse entered the room and took Catherine's pulse. After recording it in a book, she asked the young girl if she was feeling all right.

"I guess so."

The nurse turned to Hart and inquired, "Are you a relative?"

"No," answered Hart, "I'm a friend."

The nurse nodded and exited the room, leaving the two alone.

"You look terribly tired. Would you like to take a nap?" The young girl closed her eyes and didn't answer.

"I'll be in to see you tomorrow. If there is anything you want or need, have the nurse get in touch with me."

The girl gave no response as Hart stood and walked to the door. That night at dinner, Hart and Joe discussed the events of the day.

"Do you think there will be any problems?" she asked anxiously.

"Well, you know every plan has some sort of risk. The girl is uncertain about her decision...besides that, she feels insecure, vulnerable, and frightened.

This is a very ticklish situation. I just hope she doesn't back out at the last minute. Actually, this entire matter goes against my better judgement."

"I know you've agreed to all of this for my sake. I really don't think she will back out. After all, were would she go? Her boyfriend doesn't want her."

"What exactly do you know about him?"

"Only that they were seeing each other for about a year. He was employed as a chauffeur for a family on the other side of town. Apparently he wasn't earning enough to take on the responsibility of a wife, let alone a child," Hart answered with a frown. "After Catherine confessed her condition, the young man disappeared, leaving her to deal with her predicament alone. I will be very relieved when this is all over. Just think, we'll have our own little baby. We'll be a real family. Soon this will be all over."

Joe lifted his wine glass. "Here's to Catherine's beautiful, healthy baby."

"Here's to *our* beautiful, healthy baby," Hart corrected.

Later that night, Catherine gave birth to a beautiful baby boy. On the way to the hospital Hart and Joe stopped at the flower shop to choose a lovely bouquet. The couple walked through the front door of the hospital and headed straight for the stairs. Hart stuck her head in the doorway and gave a cheerful hello to the patient. Joe followed her in, feeling a bit awkward.

"How are you feeling, Catherine?"

"Oh, I'm fine—a bit tired, but otherwise I feel fine," she answered.

Hart and Joe pulled two chairs close to the bed and sat down.

"How is the baby?"

"The doctor said the baby is perfect. I only saw him for a minute. He's so beautiful." Tears welled in Catherine's eyes as she began to cry. "I hate to give him up, but I have no choice. Please take good care of him and when he asks of me, tell him that this was the hardest thing I ever had to do in my whole life!"

Joe and Hart nodded with tears in their eyes. Hart reached out and clutched the girl's hand.

"I know how difficult this must be for you, but you must remember it is all for the good of the child," Hart answered earnestly.

Later that evening, as they were preparing for bed, Joe shook his head in sadness.

"Hart, that poor girl is devastated. In a few days she will leave that hospital and her baby as well. I think it will be a long time before I will be able to forget the look on her face!"

Hart felt a touch of regret. "It doesn't seem fair that our happiness should be based on another woman's sadness. But let's not forget the most important thing—that the child will have a complete family and a good home." They held each other close. *I know we will be perfect parents,* Hart thought, as she tried to push away a twinge of guilt.

Hart found the baby was an absolute angel. She couldn't find one thing to complain about. Baby Joe was a good eater, never had a crying spell, and always slept well. With each day that passed, the couple counted their blessings, and little Joe got bigger and more beautiful. Hart loved shopping for the baby and soon he accumulated an extensive wardrobe. Although only a few months old, little Joe was extremely alert. He recognized his parents and both sets of grandparents, always smiling and waving his chubby hands. One evening Joe was balancing the baby on his knee and Hart was preparing dinner when the doorbell rang.

"I wonder who that could be?" Hart said, wiping her hands on her apron. She opened the door to find Catherine standing on the stairs with a young man beside her.

"Hello, Mrs. Allen, may we come in?"

Hart stood speechless as the young couple entered the kitchen and closed the door behind them.

"Who is it, dear?" Joe called from the parlor. Hart ignored the question as she stared at Catherine as if she were seeing a ghost.

"What do you want, Catherine? Why are you here? You agreed not to visit us. You were supposed to move out of town." Hart fought to control herself, her head spinning from the surprise visit.

"I'm sorry, Mrs. Allen, but I just couldn't do it. I couldn't forget my baby!"

"He's not your baby, for God's sake," shouted Hart. "He's ours. We've cared for him and given him love and everything else he needed. You gave him up! How dare you come back!" Hart shouted.

By then Joe had entered the kitchen holding little Joe, whose eyes were as big as saucers, alarmed at the intense conversation.

"There you are, my sweetheart," Catherine ran to Joe and took the baby from him and began rocking him and smothering him with kisses. The young man rushed over and stared at the child in awe as he put an arm around the young girl. Joe stared in disbelief at the strange tableau. Hart was crying hysterically as she rushed across the room.

"Give me that baby, right this instant!" Hart demanded between sobs.

"I'm sorry, Mrs. Allen, but I will not! This is our baby—Danny's and mine. We are going to marry after all. We want our baby—yes, *our* baby—back!" Her voice was full of determination. "We will pay you back every cent you have spent. We are leaving now, and we are taking our baby with us. I strongly suggest you do not call the police, since I am, after all, the baby's natural mother."

With that, the girl wrapped the blanket tightly around little Joe and the couple quickly left the apartment, leaving the door to slam with a resounding thud. Hart crumpled to the floor in a heap, crying uncontrollably. Joe sat next to her, holding her tightly as the silent tears rolled down his face.

"Hart... Hart, everything will be all right. We'll get him back." He held her tight as they rocked and cried together for a long, long time.

Chapter 7

The lines continually formed along City Hall Avenue and down School Street. It seemed that the word of Ponzi's business spread like wildfire through the streets of Boston. By April, 471 hopefuls left $141,670. Four times that amount of investors paid almost a half million dollars in May. By June, 7,824 people packed themselves up the dark, narrow stairway. On one particular day in the latter part of June, Ponzi claimed to have simultaneously received $500,000 and paid out $200,000. By July, he had notes outstanding with a face value of almost $15,000,000. And by this time, traffic on School Street had come to a standstill. Police were dispatched to the scene to prevent squabbles from breaking out between hot, tired, and impatient investors, many upset with some that were trying to cut in line. The Security Exchange operated daily from nine to five with some investors waiting in line for hours, but they were all very happy for they were collecting their interest and that was all that mattered to them.

Looking down from the windows of Boston's City Hall, one could see the crowd of straw hats as they bobbed down the street. Among the straws were cloth caps, women's colorful hats, and policeman's caps. The crowd grew dense as it wound its way into Pi Alley. It then flooded down City Hall Avenue, past the bank. The stream of jabbering people packed their way up the stairway of 27 School Street, wedging and shoving each other along the corridor, up the stairs, and into the office.

Ponzi sat in his chair mulling over business records. Things were going better than he had planned. *Perhaps it is greed that is sending all these people to me*, he thought. *But then, why can't everyone be rich? As long as incoming proceeds exceeded those paid out, I can continue this plan forever without buying any coupons at all! The more people that get involved, the more chance I have in succeeding. It's almost as though I am building a giant pyramid.*

He took the gold watch from his vest pocket. It was five o'clock. After snapping the lid shut, he rose from his chair and went to speak to the crowd.

"I'm sorry, everyone, but we will be closing now. Come back at nine tomorrow."

As he expected, there was a considerable amount of grumbling as the people turned and moved out of the hallway. An elderly woman muttered something about having to wait another day to become rich. One man, however, emerged from the crowd and approached Ponzi. He was a head taller and quite slender.

"Mr. Ponzi, if you have some time, I'd like to speak with you."

Ponzi shook his head. "No, I really am very busy right now. Why don't you come back to—"

"But this is really important, Mr. Ponzi," interrupted the man. "I've been keeping track of your operations, and I feel that you could do much better if you had someone to take care of your publicity, someone to spread your name to the rest of the country!"

At that moment the cream-colored limousine pulled up to the alley. Ponzi saw it and motioned for it to wait.

"Your ideas interest me, Mr—"

"Lawrence McMasters," said the man, handing Ponzi his calling card.

"...Lawrence McMasters," continued Ponzi. "I must leave now. Call me tomorrow and we'll discuss this further." He went inside.

Ponzi guessed the dumbfounded look on McMasters's face was due to the fact he was so accessible...maybe a bit too accessible, he thought. *A man of my importance should probably be more cautious of strangers. I think it might be wise to check him out.*

"Lock up for me, Tom, will you? Rose and I are going out for dinner tonight."

"Yes, sir."

Ponzi grabbed his coat and went to the car. Rose was patiently waiting inside.

"Hello, Charlie. How was your day?"

"We made $5,000 more than yesterday...you wouldn't believe how well things are going, Rose!"

Rose thought for a moment. "That's what I was going to talk to you about. Maybe there's some way I can help you at the office?" she asked hopefully.

Ponzi shook his head. "No, I want you to stay at the house. A wife's place is in the home."

She sighed. "But it's such a big house when you're not there..."

"I know, but the reason I'm in business is so you don't have to work." She appeared downcast to him. "I have a little surprise for you that might make you happy," he said, smiling.

Rose shook her finger at him sternly. "Charles Ponzi, if you bought me anything I'll—"

"No, no," he said, hardly able to contain himself. "I've decided to send for Mama. I know you'll love her, and she will keep you company when I'm working."

"That's wonderful. Oh, I can't wait to meet her!" Rose exclaimed. "What would I ever do without a fine husband like you?" she said, casting an admiring glance.

He gave her a crafty grin. "I don't know. I was wondering about that myself." They laughed as the limousine pulled up to the restaurant.

After enjoying a fine meal, the couple returned home and went directly to bed. Ponzi was beginning to find that his business was not only exciting but tiring as well.

The following morning the antique French clock chimed ten as Ponzi walked into the library. He sat down at his desk, pulled the calling card out of his coat pocket, and looked at it for a moment. A knock on the door interrupted his thoughts. The door opened and the maid looked into the room.

"Sorry to disturb you, sir, but a Mr. McMasters phoned while you were asleep. I thought you would want to know."

"Yes, Maria, thank you for telling me."

"Will you be needing anything?"

Ponzi smiled. "No, thank you."

As she shut the door behind her, Ponzi picked up the phone and dialed.

"Hello, Mr. McMasters, this is Charles Ponzi. I would like to meet with you this afternoon. How would two o'clock be?"

"Two o'clock would be fine," came the answer on the other end.

Precisely at two o'clock, Lawrence McMasters drew in a deep breath as he rang the doorbell at the Ponzi mansion. The maid opened the door and he entered the foyer. A strikingly attractive, dark-haired young woman descended the curving staircase and walked toward him as though she were floating on air.

"Hello, Mr. McMasters, I'm Rose Ponzi." She extended her hand to him, and he noticed a slight blush to her cheeks.

"It's a pleasure to meet you, Mrs. Ponzi," he said, shaking her hand. "I must say that those newspaper photos do not do you justice."

She laughed. "Oh, thank you, that's very nice of you to say. Mr. Ponzi will be down in a few minutes. Why don't you go out onto the terrace and wait for him there? Walk into the library and go straight through the French doors."

"Alright. Thank you."

A few moments later, Ponzi came outside to greet him.

"Hello, Mr. McMasters...or may I call you Larry?"

"Certainly, if I may call you Charlie!"

Ponzi let out a hearty laugh, motioned for him to sit down, and offered him a cup of coffee. McMasters accepted.

"Tell me, why do you believe I will benefit from your help?"

The public relations man smiled. "Boston knows of you, Mr. Ponzi, but I could make your name a household word. What's being printed about you now is enough to make the average reader a bit curious. However, there are ways to make the newspaper work for you, if you know what I mean."

He paused to sip his coffee. "I also have some ideas on how to spread your name to the rest of the country. Why not open branches of your company throughout the continental U.S.?"

Ponzi thought for a moment. "Yes," he agreed, shaking his head, "actually, I had thought about doing that in a year or so."

McMasters looked questioningly at him. "Why wait until then? If you were to take the right steps you would be able to accomplish that in a month or less."

"But what would I have to do?" asked Ponzi slyly.

The middle-aged man chuckled. "Now, Mr. Ponzi, if I told you that, this would probably be my last cup of coffee with you."

They both laughed again. Ponzi nodded his head and then stood.

"I think I can use you, Mr. McMasters. Come down to my office on Monday and we can talk money."

McMasters stood up, and the two shook hands. "I'm glad to see we understand each other, Mr. Ponzi. I'll let myself out the front door."

He watched his visitor leave, then finished his coffee. Rose walked out onto the terrace.

"What did the two of you talk about?"

"Mr. McMasters is going to be my publicity agent. I'll double-check his references first, but, assuming all goes well, he will help spread word about my business. He also has some good ideas, like opening other branches all over the country." He set down his cup. "Doesn't your brother live in New Jersey?"

Rose nodded. "Yes, in Newark."

"Well," he said with a smile, "he can be in charge of my first branch. We'll bring all your relatives here and they can work for me!"

She cast a fearful glance. "Charlie, I'm really worried about you. The way you treat money..."

"Rosa..."

"Sometimes I wish we were back in Somerville," she said, turning away.

Ponzi gasped. "In that broken down flat? We were poor and miserable!"

Her dark eyes widened in disbelief as she spun around. "How can you say that? We spent the happiest moments of our lives there! What does it matter where two people live, as long as they love each other?"

There was silence for a moment. Rose turned to leave, her eyes welling with tears. Ponzi grasped her hand before she could walk away from him.

"I'm sorry, Rose. I didn't mean to upset you." He turned her to him. "Don't worry about money... you'll never have to worry about money again. As far as my love for you...that, *cara mia,* will go on forever."

Her dark eyes glistened. "I love you, Charlie."

"I love you, too."

As they embraced, Rose tried to thrust the worry out of her mind. She could not help but be concerned about her husband. She loved him and did not want to lose him.

"Our life has just begun, my husband," she whispered.

She was right. Everything had just begun.

CHAPTER 8

Hart and Joe often spoke of the little baby they had lost—no, she hated that term. You lose a wallet, a shopping list, a key; you don't lose a child, at least not this one. This baby was ripped from them, and every time his name was mentioned Hart felt a dagger piercing her heart. She ached to hold him, sing to him, and rock him to sleep as she did every night. She could see his sweet angelic face, his long curly lashes and his tousled hair. And, if she tried really hard, she could smell once again the clean powdered smell that a baby possesses that made her want to smother it with kisses and hold it tightly to her breast. Hart would no longer hold little Joe, and, although they were forced to return the baby to his parents a short time ago, the emptiness they felt was so great it felt more like a lifetime. Hart and Joe agreed on one thing...when the time was right they would adopt another child, and this time they would do it the right way—everything legal, everything above board. Until then, Hart hoped Joe could get some time off from the bank, and perhaps the two of them could go away for a little while. It was no surprise that Hart was delighted when Joe suggested a short trip to "get away from it all." Her first thought was of Noddlehead, but Joe suggested a new adventure.

"How about Nantucket?" he asked.

"Nantucket? Why, I've never been there! That would be great fun."

"Good, then I'll arrange for a few days off. In the meantime, start packing!"

Three days later, Hart and Joe were on their way to catch the boat.

"Now, just promise me one thing...when we're crossing the ocean, you'll hang on to your glasses the entire time," Hart teased.

"Very funny," Joe answered.

When they docked, they found the island was dotted with sand dunes and picturesque wharves.

"This is so romantic," Hart whispered as she placed her head on Joe's shoulder. The cobblestone streets were lined with antique shops, old inns, and cottages covered with gray, weathered shingles. White picket fences surrounded most of them.

"Utterly charming," Hart murmured as they arrived at Lilac Inn. Saucer-sized blue morning glories covered the fence and climbed up the post light. Bright blue hydrangeas surrounded the house, and the yard was dotted with lovely lilac bushes and assorted flowers, their perfume drifting everywhere. While Joe took care of registering at the desk, Hart browsed through the maps and booklets on a nearby rack. The clerk selected a second floor room for the couple, and Hart purchased what appeared to be an interesting pamphlet on the island's history. In their room, they hurriedly busied themselves unpacking and making the room comfy. Hart settled in a window seat and scanned the pamphlet.

"Joe, did you know that the word 'Nantucket' is the Indian word for 'far away island?'"

"Really?"

"Yes, and Thomas Mayhew bought the island in 1646, and later sold it for thirty pounds and two beaver hats! Nantucket was in its heyday in the 1840s when the whaling industry was at its peak. It had close to 10,000 inhabitants and ninety whaling vessels, making it the greatest whaling port in the world!"

Joe sat down and lit his pipe. "This island seems so sleepy—all that seems pretty hard to believe!"

"When the whaling industry declined," Hart continued, "right around 1846, there was a great fire. People left the island in droves, leaving behind them a town untouched by factories or slums, and so it has remained, virtually unchanged for generations." She thought for a moment, then excitedly put the pamphlet down. "Let's put on our walking shoes and take a quick walk before dinner."

"Great idea."

The couple held hands as they walked the streets and drank in the quaint town. Joe peered around one corner to see wrought iron tools on exhibit. "Look, a blacksmith's shop! Let's pay him a visit and watch him work."

A man with a leather apron and sinewy arms labored arduously as he forged a piece of metal. Large beads of sweat dripped down his face as he stood before the blazing fire in the center of the barn. He turned to face the two tourists.

"Hello, folks. Enjoying your stay?"

"So far it's been wonderful," Hart answered. "Are those horseshoes you're repairing?"

"Yes, ma'am. There's a horse farm down that road where island guests can go horseback riding." The smithy pointed his finger toward a gravel road, squinting from the sun in his eyes.

"Thank you for the information—I love to ride."

Joe and Hart walked back to the Inn and found that they had returned just in time to be seated for dinner.

"We really should go up to change, Joe."

"I don't think anyone will mind if we dine casually," Joe added thoughtfully.

The dinner was delicious. Afterwards the couple retreated to the privacy of their room. The following day, Hart decided to go riding. Joe stayed behind and caught up on some reading. Hart hired a buggy to take her out to the farm and handsomely tipped the driver upon arrival. She walked through the barn and carefully inspected the horses. After choosing a spunky filly named "Fancy Face," she had her saddled and mounted her. Soon they were galloping down the dirt road, which wound around the island, through the dunes, and over the paths along the coastline. The sun was hot and Hart loved the wind blowing through her hair. It always gave her such an exhilarated feeling. She stopped the horse at the top of a knoll and looked out across the ocean. The white crests on the blue water glistened like tinsel on a Christmas tree. The gulls screamed as they dove into the water on their never-ending search for food.

"You're a great girl, Fancy Face," she whispered in the filly's ear as she stroked her head. Hart sharply pulled the reins to the right and the horse turned and broke into a full gallop beginning the long way back to the farm.

After returning to the Inn, Hart climbed out of the buggy and paid the driver. She was dusty, hot, and sticky and couldn't wait to get to her room and take a long, luxurious bath. Her face became smudged with dirt as she wiped the trickle of perspiration that had gathered at the tip of her nose.

She entered the front room and quickly began to climb the stairs. On the floor above, she heard a woman's voice gently laughing and looked up to see a distinguished-looking young lady briskly descending the stairs on the arm of none other than Bob Hutchens. Startled, Hart was completely in shock! Hutchens barely glanced at her as the couple continued their happy banter down the stairs. Hart stood frozen, her hand gripping the stair rail. *He acted as though he didn't even know me,* she thought incredulously. She turned slowly, walked downstairs, and approached the desk.

"Excuse me, but could you tell me the name of the party that just left?"

"Oh, that was Mr. and Mrs. Hutchens. Newlyweds, I understand. They certainly looked happy, didn't they?"

"Yes, they did...thank you," Hart mumbled, turning to the stairs.

Mother and Father were right—Bob didn't have any problem finding another socialite for himself, she thought. Hart entered the room and saw Joe reading in the easy chair. She closed the door rather loudly.

"Anything the matter, dear? You look a bit upset."

"No, everything is just fine. I'm going to take a long bath and relax."

"Did you have a nice ride?"

"Oh, wonderful...I just wish I had ridden a bit longer," Hart answered. She went over and planted a kiss on Joe's forehead and headed for the bathroom to draw her bath.

Rising early the next morning, the couple went down to the dining room for breakfast. To Hart's relief, the room was empty, but every time the front door opened Hart expected to see Bob and his wife appear. Fortunately, breakfast was uneventful. As they walked by the front desk, the clerk called out, "Mr. and Mrs. Allen, I hoped I could introduce you to the happy honeymooners, but they suddenly decided to leave this morning."

"Oh, what a shame," Hart answered, secretly relieved. "I wonder why?"

The rest of the vacation breezed by, and soon Hart and Joe were on their way home.

Chapter 9

Ponzi's office manager sat down at the kitchen table and let out a sigh. Working for Ponzi had become a hellish nightmare. It seemed like a year, not a few months, since Ponzi had hired him. He quickly scanned the front page as he hurried through his breakfast.

"Tom, for goodness sake, can't you just once take your time and enjoy what I put in front of you?" his mother asked with a grim expression on her face.

"Ma, we've gone through this a million times! I have to hurry and try to beat the crowd at the office."

"A million this and a million that...don't you talk in hundreds anymore?" His mother switched to Italian and continued to rant, but Tom automatically tuned her out. The headlines on the front page captured his attention: "NEW AGENTS ADDED TO PONZI'S EMPLOY TO HELP WITH OVERLOAD."

"Great, that's just what we need!" The constant pressure was beginning to show on the young man. So much had happened in a few short months—it was incomprehensible how Ponzi's idea had caught on the way it did.

"Will you be home for supper?" His mother's sharp voice abruptly brought him back to the present.

"Yeah, I guess so, Ma. If not, save it for me."

Tom grabbed the paper, downed the last of his coffee, and rushed out the door and down the stairs. Outside, the temperature was already in the 80s.

Walking a good pace would get him to School Street in about twelve minutes. As he rounded the last street corner, his biggest fear became a reality. The worst run had commenced, with more than 500 investors all anxiously waiting to give or get their money. A detail of police officers were doing their best to keep the crowd in an orderly line, which was backed up to City Hall and constantly expanding. Ponzi's company offered hot dogs and coffee for the long line seeking to get their money back.

Tom pushed his way through the crowd and opened the door amid a roar of cheers from those waiting in the hot sun. He allowed a group of about twenty people to enter, and they quickly climbed the stairs to be swiftly served by the waiting clerks in their cages. Tom ran to his station just as the phone began ringing.

"Hello, Security Exchange."

"Tom, this is Mr. Ponzi. Is everything under control?"

"Well, barely, sir. We're having another huge run this morning. Do you have any instructions?"

"Just keep everything on an even keel. I'll be there later today." Ponzi hung up the phone and called Rose. "The cameraman will be here soon. Check if Mama is ready and if the staff has prepared the house for filming. I want everything to be perfect!"

As he completed the sentence, the doorbell rang and the butler showed the camera crew inside. Ponzi and his family were to pose for the movies.

"Hello and welcome!" Charlie grandly bowed and gestured for the small group to join him in the study. "How wonderful to have you as guests in my home. Please, make yourselves comfortable. My wife and mother will join us soon." After a few minutes, Rose and her mother-in-law entered the room dressed in their finest clothes and jewels.

"Ah, Rose...Mama! The newsmen are here to film us."

Rose looked radiant in a crimson dress, her hair held in a bun at the top of her head. Her neck and wrists sparkled with diamonds. The elder Mrs. Ponzi wore a black lace dress that touched the floor, and a black ribbon tied around her neck displayed a huge diamond brooch. The family was filmed at the dining room table being served caviar by the staff, and then in the library examining the book-lined shelves and the valuable art collection that adorned the walls.

The director of the film crew clamored for more. "How about a few scenes of the three of you relaxing?"

"Fine, let's go out to the garden and play a bit of croquet," Ponzi suggested, thoroughly enjoying his brief stint at acting. The group proceeded to the rose garden and played through a few shots while cameras rolled.

"I think we have enough footage, Mr. Ponzi," said the director. "Thank you for allowing us to see what a day in the life of Charles Ponzi is like!"

"When will this news special be released?"

"I guess it will be in the theater in four to five days. We'll give you a call as soon as it's out."

"Wonderful...wonderful! Thank you so much, and good day!"

Later that week the Ponzi family occupied a box in the theater and immensely enjoyed the news footage of themselves at work and play. Charlie mysteriously excused himself from his wife and mother and went backstage. The curtain opened to reveal the stage set with a scene of Ponzi's office. Ponzi was sitting at a desk while a bit actor worked by his side playing the part of an office boy. Moments later a man came in the door and walked up to Ponzi's desk.

"Yes, Mr. Ponzi, I'd like to invest one million dollars."

Charlie wrote out a note and gave it to the man. The man walked out the door and a moment later walked back in and collected one and a half million dollars. The theater crowd cheered and Charlie took a deep bow. He looked up to the box seats, waving and throwing a kiss to a surprised but delighted Rose and Mama. This caused the crowd to cheer even louder. Ponzi was satisfied with his performance and the audience's response. "Thank you, ladies and gentlemen. I always wanted to be an actor!" *I'm so glad I'm such a good one*, he thought.

Chapter 10

Hart heard the door to the apartment close and Joe's footsteps coming down the hall. She called out to him.

"Everything all right? You're home early."

"It's more than all right—it's splendid!"

"What is it? What's happened?"

"Read this," he said as he held out an envelope.

Hart quickly removed the letter and slowly read the contents. Her eyes widened as she scanned the last paragraph:

```
"Therefore, as Governor of the State of
Massachusetts, I hereby appoint you Bank
Commissioner of Massachusetts. I have
great confidence that you will execute
this position using your sound judgment,
honesty, and keen banking knowledge to the
best of your ability."

Respectfully,
Calvin Coolidge, Governor
```

Hart stared wide-eyed at her husband.

"Oh, my word! I can't believe it!"

Joe looked down at her sheepishly. "There was talk of it, Hart, but I didn't want to say anything until it was definite."

"I am so proud of you!" She pulled him to her and kissed him hard.

"I am married to the most wonderful woman in the world," he whispered in her ear.

"And you, my dear sir, are a flatterer," she answered, looking adoringly into his eyes.

In one swoop he picked her up and carried her to the bedroom, carefully depositing her on the bed. He pulled her to him and slowly opened the buttons on her blouse.

The following day, the couple began checking the newspapers for an apartment.

"Well, as long as we can find something fairly decent, it doesn't have to be permanent. After all, we do want to buy a house," Joe assured her.

After checking several possibilities, they found an ad for an apartment in a fairly decent section of Boston. "I'll check it out tomorrow," Joe said.

The next morning, after traveling to Boston, Joe found the house and checked the ad he had brought along with him. "Apartment for rent, ask for Helen," he read out loud. He climbed the stairs and quickly rang the doorbell. Inside, Helen peeked through the window and watched as the distinguishably dressed man straightened his tie and waited for someone to answer the door. Glancing at herself in the hall mirror, she pulled a loose lock of hair up and carefully moistened her lips. *He certainly looks interesting*, she thought as she pulled open the door.

"Hello," the stranger greeted her with a friendly smile. "I'd like to speak to Helen regarding the apartment for rent."

"Of course…come in, I'm Helen." She tried to sound as sophisticated as he looked.

"My name is Joseph Allen. My wife and I are interested in the upstairs apartment...is it still available?"

"It certainly is—may I show it to you?" she asked with a smile.

"Yes, by all means."

Helen reached for the keys lying on the shelf and stepped outside. As the two climbed the stairs, Helen was happy she was wearing her tightest dress.

"It's a lovely, bright apartment, Mr. Allen. I'm sure you'll find everything you need, and if you don't, just let me know—I'll be right downstairs," she said with a promising twinkle in her eye.

Joe cleared his throat. "Ah...yes, thank you. It does appear to be a fine place," Joe answered, a bit embarrassed. "My wife saw your ad in the paper, and the monthly rental is certainly acceptable."

Helen showed Joe around, and when the two returned to the kitchen Helen asked, "Well, what do you think? Would you like to take it?" placing her hands on her hips.

"Yes, I think it will do fine. I'll give you the first month's rent in advance."

"Wonderful," she purred as she took the bills and stuffed them into her pocket.

Later that afternoon, after being escorted to a table at Sharkey's, Helen sat down, crossed her legs, and lit a cigarette. She leaned forward, exposing her ample breasts.

"I tell you, Rocky, just when I thought I'd met all kinds, this guy shows up and proves me wrong! He's rich, but stuffy...real stuffy! I can just imagine what his wife must be like. But hey, what the hell, as long as he has the bucks for the apartment, right?"

"Who's that, angel?" her hefty, dark-haired friend asked in a low voice.

"The stuffed shirt I'm renting the apartment to, dummy!" Helen shouted. "Jesus Christ, don't you pay attention to anything I say?"

"Yeah, sure I do, but I got more important things on my mind," Rocky grumbled.

"Well, anyway, he's a rich guy. I could tell by his clothes. His name is Joseph Allen and he works for some bank," Helen confided.

"A bank man? Guess you won't have to worry about the rent being regular," he shot back with a toothy grin.

"You're not shittin' there, honey!" Helen answered with a low chuckle as she took a puff and blew out a perfect smoke ring.

Rocky downed his drink, kissed Helen on the cheek, and made a quick exit. Something big was up and he didn't want to be late for the meeting. After making a mad run for the warehouse, he hurried up the two flights of stairs, rushed into the outer office, and quickly took a seat. He tried to stop the strangled feeling he was getting from his tie by pulling his collar loose. Beads of perspiration gathered on his forehead and slowly trickled down the side of his face. He took out his handkerchief, mopped his brow, and stole a curious look at Marco, who was seated next to him.

"What the hell is takin' so long?" he whispered hoarsely.

"The boss ain't too happy with the last job Tony did."

The two men strained to hear the low conversation in the next room, which was occasionally peppered with sudden outbursts.

"Jesus, boss, I'm sorry. I tell you it won't happen again!" Tony could be heard pleading his case.

"Make very sure it don't, Tony, because next time you'll be six feet under. You got that?"

"Yah, boss...thanks...thanks a lot!" The door opened and Tony slipped out looking scared shitless as he made a fast exit.

Rocky and Marco stood up and slowly filed into the room.

"Sit down, boys," the boss ordered. Both men obediently dropped into leather chairs opposite the large mahogany desk.

"I hear on the streets that Ponzi is really raking in the dough. I like that! It's good to see a fellow *compare* doing well. It makes me proud. You know what I mean?" demanded the well-dressed man with the white carnation in his lapel. "I even invested a little wad with the guy myself! It looks good to our people, you know?" The man rose from the desk and began to slowly pace around the room, puffing on his cigar. "Last month Ponzi had his foot in the door of the Hanover Bank, and now he's got his whole goddamn ass in there. That sonofabitch is practically running the joint. Hell, he's got that goddamn bank president eatin' out of his hands!" He laughed heartily. "Now, here's what I want from you guys. I want you both to do a little snoopin' and find out if anyone in particular is out to get him. I want to know about any poor bastard that doesn't like what Charlie's doin', and I want to know *right away*!" The boss man jabbed his finger in the air.

Rocky answered for himself and Marco. "OK, boss, you bet! We'll get right on it."

Both men stood up and waited for their dismissal.

"By the way, Rocky, how's that girl of yours? What's her name...Helen?"

"Oh, she's fine, boss," Rocky answered, curious about the question.

"You better keep your eye on her, Rocky, 'cause she's nice...real nice."

Rocky got ticked off at the comment, but reminded himself not to be an asshole and kept his mouth shut.

"OK, boys, that's all. Let me know as soon as you hear anything," was the final order.

Rocky and Marco walked silently down the stairs. Rocky was still boiling mad about the remark the boss made about Helen. Out on the sidewalk both men decided to canvas a different part of the city and meet in two hours to discuss their findings. Rocky decided to pass by Ponzi's headquarters on School Street and see what he could dig up. Even at this hour the crowd was huge as usual. Rocky noticed one of his buddies waiting in line.

"Angelo! What the hell are *you* doin' here?" he asked, slapping his buddy across the back.

"Hey, Rock, how the hell are ya?"

"You waitin' to give this guy Ponzi your gamblin' money?"

"You're goddamn right I am! The guy is getting everyone rich, so why the hell shouldn't I?"

Rocky noticed a policeman in the crowd nearby, so he lowered his voice.

"Have you heard anything new about this guy?"

"Yeah. Some guy named McMasters who works for Ponzi says he may be a candidate for Governor of Massachusetts!"

"You're shittin' me."

"Hey, I wouldn't shit you, Rock. This guy's a genius. If my old man is willin' to mortgage the house, then I'll take a chance, too!"

Rocky playfully punched the guy in the arm. "You're a hot shit, Angelo! Say hi to the old man and the old lady for me. Tell her someday I'm gonna surprise her and stop in for some pasta and her great sauce!"

Angelo smiled. "You bet, Rock, I'll tell her, and ya know what she's gonna say: 'Tell that Rocky he's always welcome in our house!'"

"I can hear her already!" Rocky laughed.

Rocky continued down the street and stepped in the door of the Hanover Bank. He noticed a shiny new plaque on the wall that named Ponzi as one of the bank directors. The directory listed an office for Ponzi on the second floor, across the hall from the bank president.

"Jesus Christ, the boss was right. I wish to hell I knew this guy's secret," he muttered, shaking his head.

Rocky left the bank considering if he, too, should invest with this so-called genius. *Hey, what the hell, if it's good enough for the boss, it's good enough for me,* he thought as he went back to School Street and fell in line with the others. *Two hundred bucks won't break me. Jesus, in forty-five days I'll get my money back with fifty percent interest. Then I can buy Helen something really nice!* Helen...he began to wonder what the hell she was doing now. Actually, on second thought, he wasn't sure he really wanted to know.

Almost automatically, he found his feet taking him to Helen's apartment.

Rocky rang the doorbell, impatiently tapping his foot as he waited for Helen to answer. The door slowly opened, and Helen peeked out.

"Rocky, what are you doing here? I wasn't expecting you!"

"Yeah, I know that, I thought I'd surprise you." Rocky pushed past Helen and let himself into the apartment.

"So, whatcha' been doin' lately?" Rocky asked with a curious look as he dropped into a chair.

"Oh, nothing special," Helen quickly replied as she nervously brushed the hair off her forehead. Rocky was quite familiar with that nervous habit of hers.

He noticed the glittery bracelet on Helen's wrist.

"Where'd the rocks come from? I never saw them before." Rocky's eyes became two thin slits as he stared at Helen, waiting for her answer.

"It's not new, Rocky...I've had it for a long time," Helen stammered.

A sharp sound filled the room as Rocky slapped Helen across the face. Helen reeled from the force of the blow, and when she straightened up and faced him a thin line of blood trickled from one of her nostrils.

"Don't you lie to me, you little bitch! What do you think I am, stupid or somethin'?"

"No, honest, Rocky, it's the truth," Helen whimpered.

Rocky gave her a shove, and she fell into the chair behind her.

"You had better not be screwing around behind my back, or I'm gonna break your neck," he threatened, shaking his fist.

"I won't...I promise." The drop of blood under her nostril had now become a long red line down to her chin.

"Get me a drink...I'm thirsty," he demanded with a growl. Helen jumped up and hurried to the kitchen to do his bidding. She poured a drink as she wiped the blood off her quivering face. Looking in the kitchen mirror she could see her lip swelling.

"That bastard is going to pay for this," she quietly hissed as she spit into his drink. In the living room Rocky had removed his coat and shoes.

Helen hurried in and placed the drink on the table beside him.

"Thanks, doll, that's much better. Now, how about tellin' me where you got the bracelet?"

"It's no big deal, Rocky. I saved a few months' rent and treated myself to a piece of jewelry. Any crime against that?"

"No," Rocky answered in a low voice, "as long as that's what happened!"

"Now, Rock, you know I'd never lie to you," Helen purred.

"Oh, yeah? Just remember that, in case you're ever tempted." *I know she's lyin' to me*, he thought. *But who is she screwin' around with?*

"So...have you seen the boss lately?"

"Now why would you ask me that?" Helen's face flushed.

"Oh, no reason...I just had a feelin' you might have forgotten to tell me about it."

Helen tried to compose herself. "Well, I did see him a few days ago...at the club...but that was just for a few minutes. In fact, he asked about you."

"Really? That's funny, he asked me about you, too!" Rocky studied Helen's expression, trying to read between the lines. "You know what I do to bimbos who cheat on me? They end up taking a long walk off a short pier."

Helen slid her arm around Rocky's neck. "Come on, Rocky! I'd never do that to you!"

He looked deep into her eyes, and, in a low voice, whispered, "It's a good thing, babe, 'cause you're too beautiful to end up as fish bait."

Helen turned away and walked slowly to the kitchen. *I think I better talk to Sam*, she thought to herself. It was funny how quickly she had gotten on a first name basis with the boss. *He's big time, not small potatoes like Rocky.* One word from her and Rock would be a memory! The corner of her lips turned up as she savored her newly-found power.

"Want another drink?" she asked casually.

"No thanks—and don't change the subject," Rocky growled.

"Oh, calm down, will you? For Chrissakes, stop being so paranoid!" Helen yelled. "What the hell? Just because someone asked about me doesn't mean we were in the sack together!" Helen loved playing up the innocent routine. *Just put him on the defensive*, she thought. *It always works.*

"Alright, alright, calm down," Rocky bellowed. "I just wanted to warn you ahead of time. How about gettin' all dolled up and we'll go out to the club for a while before it closes?"

"Oh, I can't, Rock...I've got an awful headache, and I still have a fat lip, see?"

"Okay then, I'll go by myself. I'll be by to see you tomorrow," he shot back as he walked out the door.

Chapter 11

Joe and Hart celebrated their first month in their new apartment by going out to dinner at a little Italian restaurant a few blocks away. The waiter served the couple two steaming platters of pasta, and with exaggerated flair he opened a bottle of wine, pouring a little into each glass. Hart smiled at Joe and raised her glass.

"Here's to happy days in our new apartment," she toasted.

"Hear, hear," he agreed as their two glasses clinked in midair.

The couple dug into their dinner with gusto, enjoying the food and the Italian opera arias that played on the old Victrola in the background. Hart noticed Joe watching the entrance and her eyes followed his. A well-dressed man with a carnation in his lapel stood at the door surrounded by several other surly looking men. The owner rushed over to the new arrivals and welcomed them nervously but warmly. He quickly led three of them to a table in a dark corner of the room and signaled for a waiter. One man stayed behind at the door.

"Now who do you suppose that man is with the flower?" Hart asked.

"I'm not sure...but I have a few ideas."

Hart continued to eat, but occasionally stole a peek at the interesting party. After wiping his mouth with his napkin Joe placed it on the table.

"I have a hunch they could be involved with the mob."

Hart was surprised at Joe's remark. "Oh, my! Really?"

At that moment, the owner of the restaurant turned the sign on the door over and closed the establishment for the evening.

"Well, for heaven's sake," Hart whispered. "Did you see that? I guess they must be important!"

After finishing their dinner in silence, the couple paid their bill and walked to the door. Joe gave a smile and a curt nod to the man standing there, but the man's sullen expression did not change as he opened the door for the couple. As they exited, Hart and Joe passed a short and flamboyantly dressed man who went inside.

"Ah, Roberto, good evening. I've come to join some friends for dinner. Am I too late?"

"No, Charlie, they just arrived," called the owner as he hurriedly ushered the dapper new arrival to the mysterious gathering inside. When he neared the table, the man with the carnation rose.

"Eh! *Paisane*! Charlie Ponzi! It's a pleasure to finally meet ya!" exclaimed the man.

He shook Ponzi's hand so firmly Charlie feared it would fall off.

"The pleasure is all mine. Thank you for your gracious invitation to dinner," said Ponzi, gritting his teeth in pain.

The man realized Ponzi's discomfort. "Oh, I'm so sorry. Sometimes I don't know my own strength! Forgive me, please. Sit down and join us. Roberto, my friend, bring us over a bottle of your finest, all right?"

The owner scurried over with a bottle of wine and bread. He poured a glass each for the gathered group.

"Charlie, I invited ya here because I'm a big fan of yours," said the boss man.

Ponzi smiled again. "That's very nice."

"Ya know, there are some people in Boston that aren't too happy with what you're doin'. They're complainin' you're cutting into their action. Some of the other bosses, that is, but not *me*. I tell 'em, 'Hey, leave Charlie alone. He's making a decent livin' and he's helpin' out all his investors, too!' Know what I mean?"

A large tray of antipasto arrived. One of the men at the table hungrily reached in with a fork for some prosciutto. The boss man angrily slapped the man's fork down.

"Marco, what the hell are you doing? Where's your manners? Let our guest here get his fork in there first!" the boss yelled. Marco put his fork down and gingerly rubbed his hand. The boss turned back to Ponzi. "I apologize for Marco's behavior, Charlie. He ain't got no manners."

Ponzi didn't flinch at the outburst and tried to calm the mood back down. "It's all right, I'm only going to have something light—maybe just some pasta with a little sauce." Roberto brought over butter for the bread. The boss's mood lightened immediately and rather suddenly. "Hey, Charlie, have you ever tried Roberto's clam sauce? It's the best in town, I'm tellin' ya. I don't know what he puts in it, but it's really somethin'. It stays with you hours afterwards." He turned slightly apologetically to Roberto, who wore a quizzical expression. "I don't mean that in a bad way, Roberto."

Roberto nodded with a look of relief.

Ponzi's curiosity was getting the better of him. He tried to ask a question without showing the fear that was rising in his gut. "You say some bosses are mad at me. What do you think they'll do?"

"They're not gonna do nothin', Charlie," assured the boss. "I'll make sure of that. I told 'em to let the numbers racket go for a while and start investin' with you. I said, 'This guy knows what he's doing, so do as I do and back him up.' I even invested some money with ya, too, Charlie." The boss looked over at the fourth man at the table. "I'm trying to get my boy Rocky over here to back ya, but he's blowin' all his dough on that hot gal of his."

Rocky smiled. "Yeah, boss—well, I may not be blowin' it on her too much longer."

"That's good, Rock, 'cause she ain't worth it," replied the boss. "Believe you me."

"So what do you want from me?" Ponzi interrupted nervously.

The boss laughed. "Charlie, my friend, you misunderstan'. I don't want *nothin'* from you. I told ya, I think you're great. I'm happy just knowin' ya. You're famous, for Chrissakes. Everybody was jealous when they heard that we was havin' dinner together tonight—me and the great Ponzi! Don't worry. I don't need *nothin'*. I'm just watching that nobody tries to stop what you're doin'. Consider it a gift from a fellow '*paisane*.' That's the only real gift you might need. You sure as hell don't need any money, that's for sure. Right, boys?" The men chuckled at the table as dinner arrived.

Chapter 12

Joe took Hart's hand as they started the short walk home.

"You know, one of those men looked familiar," Hart said in a low voice. "I believe he's one of Helen's suitors. He's been to the house a few times. I'm almost positive."

"I thought so," Joe answered. "It would be interesting to know just how much Helen is involved with those people. I don't like the idea of living under the same roof with anyone connected with those shady characters!"

"Nor do I, dear!" Hart began to think. "Perhaps we should start looking for a home of our own."

"That's an excellent idea! Why don't you look into that tomorrow, Hart?"

"I certainly will!"

The following morning Hart called and spoke with several realtors, checking on sizes, prices, and distances to churches, schools, and stores. Although Joe had cautioned her to stay within their budget, he had also indicated he would be willing to see any house Hart found especially appealing.

Early the next morning, Hart's pulse raced with excitement. *House-hunting will be a new experience for me, and I do love new experiences*, she thought.

After her first appointment, Hart felt disappointed at the house she had just toured. She found it had a tiny kitchen, little closet space, and a large price tag. She decided to stop in a restaurant, looking forward to the bit of free time sandwiched in between her appointments. On the way, she noticed a lovely little house with a "for sale" sign on the front lawn, so she stopped and made a note of the location on her map. Hart ordered her lunch and watched as the waiter delivered her coffee and salad.

"Enjoying your afternoon, ma'am?" the waiter asked.

"Actually, I'm house-hunting, which is not an easy chore," Hart answered with exasperation.

"Are you having any luck?"

"I'm afraid not, though I did notice a lovely little cottage on my walk back here."

"Oh? Where was it located?"

Hart showed him the street on her map.

The waiter scratched his head and frowned. "I don't think you want that house!"

"Why not?"

"Well...umm, you see..." he stammered, trying to choose the right words, "...that's what we call the 'Red Light' district," he blurted out loudly.

Several people in the restaurant turned and looked at Hart. She quickly buried her head in the menu, her face flushed with embarrassment as the waiter hurried back to the kitchen.

Her house-hunting trip proved to be fruitless. Hart returned to the apartment a bit disappointed, but not yet ready to give up. "The right house will come along sooner or later," she told her husband. "We'll just have to keep looking."

Hart was thrilled when Joe suggested they see a house he had heard about in Newton Highlands.

"I think we should check this house out. I would feel much better knowing you were safe and sound in our own home. I think the timing is right, especially if we are considering adding a child to our family someday."

"You are absolutely right!" Hart agreed.

The following morning Joe and Hart were on the road to Newton Highlands. Hart enjoyed the scenic drive, but Joe's mind was still on business matters.

"The governor called me yesterday. It seems he's quite concerned with what is happening to the banking business in Massachusetts. Apparently that man Ponzi is giving several of our banks a bit of competition. We've been watching him for the past few months and there's something fishy going on."

"Really?"

"Since he started his business, it seems thousands of people have withdrawn huge amounts of money from the banks to invest with this dreamer. I've been asked to pay a visit to the Hanover Bank and see what's going on there. Coolidge wants a report on my findings."

"You know, everyone is talking about this," Hart said thoughtfully. "Isn't he that Italian man who says he wants to make everyone a millionaire? When I was house-hunting, there was a terrible traffic jam, and when I asked the cabdriver what was going on, he said 'Santa Claus' was holding court. How can people be so gullible?"

"Everyone wants to believe there's an easy way to getting rich, so they'll try anything!" Joe answered.

The car turned down Norman Road and the couple checked the numbers on the houses. "There it is—that brown bungalow across the street!" Hart exclaimed.

Joe stopped the car and the two of them got out and looked around.

"Isn't this a lovely place?" Hart asked happily. The house was neat-looking and seemed in good repair. About two hundred yards from the property the glistening waters of a lake shone through the trees. Hart and Joe walked the grounds, carefully inspecting the area. They then went to the back door and Joe withdrew a key from his coat pocket.

"Bob Simons is being transferred. He gave me a key so we could look over the house and let him know if we'd be interested in purchasing it."

As they stepped into the kitchen, Hart noticed how spacious it was. A cozy breakfast nook took up an entire corner of the room. They walked through the hall and into the living room.

"Oh, I love large windows, Joe. They make the house so bright and cheerful." She paused to admire the view. "Doesn't the lake look absolutely beautiful from here?" Joe nodded in agreement as he put his arm around Hart's shoulders. After going from room to room, they both knew it was the house for them.

"Is there a second floor?" Hart asked.

"No, there's just an attic. Bob said it could easily be converted into an extra bedroom."

Hart smiled. "I love it...let's buy it!"

"I'll tell Bob as soon as we get back!" Joe said, catching her excitement.

"I just can't wait to move in—I know we're going to be so happy here." Hart squeezed Joe's arm as they drove down the road. She took a last peek at the house through the rear window.

"We can call Mother and tell her we will finally be taking our belongings out of her attic. It'll be wonderful to be able to use all those lovely wedding gifts! It's about time, wouldn't you say?"

Looking over at Hart, Joe smiled and nodded his approval.

CHAPTER 13

Ponzi leaned back in his chair and took a puff on his expensive cigar. His decision to open offices all over New England was a brilliant move. As more and more agents were hired to cope with the tremendous expansion of his business, Charlie had decided to cut each one in with ten percent of their take. At this point, he was told many agents had taken on agents because they were swamped with clients.

"Lucy, take this letter," Ponzi ordered his secretary.

```
Dear Sir:

You are invited to a meeting to discuss
a subject I think you will find of great
importance. I have decided to organize
a two hundred million dollar corporation
with a chain of  "profit sharing banks"
in which depositors will share with
stockholders in the net profit. Please
join me, along with a distinguished
group of well-known financiers, to discuss
this plan at length. Everyone attending
will be my guest for the weekend.

Respectfully yours,
Charles Ponzi
```

"Make twenty copies of that letter and send one to each person on this list," Charlie told the young woman as he handed her a sheet of paper.

"Yes, sir," she replied as she turned on her heels and quickly left the room. Ponzi thought about how far he had come. He had already bought into the Hanover Trust, where only months ago he had made his first meager deposit. Recently, he had been appointed a member of the board of directors of that same bank. In fact, he blew a circle of smoke above his head from a cigar someone had named after him! Ponzi picked up the *Boston Post* and saw his name spread across the front page.

"In the headlines, again," he mumbled to himself.

The assistant publisher of the *Post*, Richard Grozier, was beginning to get on his nerves. Ponzi was aware that some people were running a crusade against him. First they had suggested that Charlie had not bought one dime's worth of International Coupons. Today, to his surprise, Ponzi read that the *Post* was curious why he would deposit his money in a bank that only paid five per cent when his business was paying fifty per cent to other people. Snuffing out his cigar, he rose and looked out his office window. At that moment he spotted his touring car winding its way through the crowded streets to the office door. He watched as Rose waited patiently for him. Charlie picked up his gold-headed Malacca cane and straw hat and walked to the door. *I think I will call a press conference for later this week*, he thought as he opened the door. *My public will need some encouragement.*

The following day, Ponzi called the Security Exchange Office. Tom answered. "I'm going to be in a little later on, Tom. Open up around nine o'clock as usual."

The clerk peered out through the window behind his work area.

"People have been here since seven, Mr. Ponzi. There's a big crowd outside right now—I'd say at least 300 people. The police are trying to keep order, but I don't know how long it will last..."

"Tell them that we will open for general business on Thursday, do you understand?"

The clerk nodded. "Yes, sir, I'll do that." He hung up the phone and went back to sorting money. He heard the door buzzer and went to let in a fellow clerk. The young man looked disheveled as he entered the small office.

"It's a madhouse out there," he exclaimed. Tom chuckled. The other clerk became annoyed.

"What the hell are you laughing about? Those people almost took me apart!"

"Just be thankful you're in here and not waiting out there for your money. It will be a lot worse by the time we open," said Tom as he walked over to peer at the thermometer. "Look at that! It's only 8:45 and the temperature in here is already seventy-five degrees."

"I don't know about that bastard Ponzi, making us work in this sweat shop," said the clerk. He was obviously not pleased with the office that Ponzi had set up for his employees.

Ponzi and his secretary at least have desks, thought Tom. In his opinion, the least that an employer could do would be to make the surroundings a little more comfortable. Tom had seen Ponzi's plush office at the Hanover Bank and knew that he could well afford to give his employees better working conditions.

These thoughts were interrupted by the harsh shrill of the buzzer.

"Someday I'm going to disconnect that goddamn thing," Tom said half-aloud.

He let in another clerk and one of Ponzi's secretaries.

Soon it was nine o'clock and it was opening time. Tom peeked out the window. Pi Alley looked like the midway of Barnum's Circus. The crowd was tremendous. There were at least 500 people out there as the crowd made its way to School Street.

He went downstairs and asked the policeman how long the line was.

"What line? We got them in a line here, but it's a different story on City Hall Avenue."

Tom gasped. City Hall Avenue!

The officer looked at Tom again. "This was a goddamn good idea Mr. Ponzi had, but when will it all stop?"

"Stop?" Another officer had joined in the conversation. "Who the hell would want it to stop?" He had a good point which no one could argue.

Tom spoke again. "We're opening up now." The policeman nodded and backed the line up a bit. Tom came out from behind the door and stood on a wooden crate, which, along with the bushel baskets, had become a Ponzi trademark. The throng quieted down some when they saw Tom.

"Ladies and Gentlemen," he began, like a Master of Ceremonies speaking to his audience, "we are now open..." The resulting cheers drowned out the rest of his sentence, and the din surprised him. He didn't want to say what he would have to say next.

"Mr. Ponzi has asked me to inform you that all offices and branches will be closed tomorrow, and will reopen for regular business on Thursday." The crowd was not happy with that bit of news. Tom became nervous when a few booed. Public speaking was not one of his talents. Several reporters pushed their way up to the front.

"When will Ponzi make a statement to the press?" asked one.

Tom spoke loudly so he could be heard over the noise of the crowd. "Mr. Ponzi will be here a little later this morning." He looked at one of the policeman who had spoken with him a few minutes ago. "Would you let in the first ten or fifteen?"

Tom walked back upstairs and into the office.

It was business as usual that morning. Tom knew that Ponzi had collected a lot of money, but he couldn't help wondering whether his boss was losing a lot from this morning's run on withdrawals.

Later on that day the cream-colored limousine pulled up. The police made room for it, and the Japanese driver got out and opened the door for the great Ponzi. With cocky manner and bouncing step, he exited the vehicle, as usual impeccably dressed from his pointed shoes to his razor sharp creased pants, all the way up to his straw hat. He wore a pearl stick pin in his silk tie and a boutonniere in his lapel.

Ponzi smiled and tipped his hat and the crowd hushed. Pulling out a certified check from behind the handkerchief in his coat pocket, he held it up in the air for all the crowd to see. "Do not fear, you will all get your money just as I have promised," he shouted confidently.

The reporters pushed their way through again. "Mr. Ponzi, is there anything else you can tell the people?"

Ponzi thought hard. What could he tell the public, the investors who could decide his fate? He smiled the trademark Ponzi smile.

"Well, first of all, I would like to say that I have no idea what my liabilities are and I don't care." The crowd quieted. "I have plenty of money to meet them," he added.

"I can lay my hands on $7,500,000 in this country at any moment. And that figure does not include securities in vaults or real estate. I have also received an offer of a like sum from a Canadian bank."

These words took the crowd by surprise. It gave everyone a feeling of even greater security. Their respect for the man was sure to increase. "How much money did you pay out so far?" asked another reporter. Ponzi took out a sheet of paper from his briefcase and looked at it.

"I have paid out $418,522 to note-holders yesterday, which brings the total since last Tuesday to between $4,000,000 and $4,500,000."

"What are your plans for the future?" asked yet another of the many reporters pumping Ponzi for as much information to print as possible. He turned to him.

"I plan to form an organization capitalized at $100,000,000 and eventually $200,000,000, the investors in which will receive a conservative monthly interest plus extra dividends quarterly, semi-annually, yearly, or from time to time. The capital I'll eventually attract will be used to promote industrial enterprise."

His statement was unexpected. There were scattered cheering from those who could grasp the amount of money he was talking about, but after a few seconds the whole crowd began to join in. *They would cheer at anything,* Ponzi thought. He continued his speech.

"They will not break me today," he said, "and I promise they will not do it tomorrow!"

"How do your employees feel about your ability to reimburse all your note holders?" asked a man nearby.

Tom wished he hadn't asked that question. Ponzi was about to say something, but decided to put his clerk on the spot. "I think that Tom can answer that better than I can." He put his arm around Tom and looked at him.

Tom swallowed nervously. "We are confident as ever that Mr. Ponzi will be able to meet all demands." Ponzi smiled at Tom and gave him a pat on the back. Tom gave a wan smile in return.

Just then a loud voice came from somewhere in the crowd. "You are the greatest Italian that ever lived!" shouted someone, obviously one of Ponzi's biggest fans.

"No, the third greatest," Ponzi laughingly shot back. "You forget Columbus and Marconi. The first discovered America, Marconi discovered the wireless, and—"

"—and you discovered money," shouted the unabashed admirer. The crowd erupted into huge cheers. A smile spread across Ponzi's face.

Ponzi spoke up again. "Thank you for your time, gentlemen," he said to the reporters. The crowd continued cheering loudly as he waved. He saw an old woman in line who was waiting to cash in her note and thought of Mama. "Come with me," he called, and guided the woman in so she could get her investment immediately.

The reporters left, wondering how much longer they would have to visit this place. Although by now his investors consisted of lawyers, judges, policemen, and politicians, Ponzi was able to temporarily bury the rumor that he could not pay off!

Hart-Lester Harris Allen on her wedding day, December 21, 1918.

A photo of a charcoal drawing of Hart by an unknown artist.

Charles Ponzi in 1920

Rose Gnecco Ponzi, date unknown

Joe Allen holding Covington, Hart and Joe's second adopted son.

Hart and Joe pause for a photo while on their honeymoon.

Joe and Hart's house on Norman Road in Newton Highlands, MA, nicknamed the 'Brown Bungalow."

The Harris residence in Springfield, MA, Hart's childhood home.

The Harris summer residence on Chebeague Island, ME, nicknamed "Noddlehead."

Hart posing at Chebeague, ME, date unknown.

Joseph Allen's publicity photo as Massachusetts Commissioner of Banks.

Hart-Lester Harris at Smith College, 1913

Hart-Lester Harris at Smith College, 1913

Roy and Jeannie Gionfriddo with Hart-Lester Allen

The authors giving Hart a card and present on her birthday in 1973. L-R: Mark (partially hidden), Jeannie and daughter Tina, Hart.

Chapter 14

Ponzi looked through his records and leaned back in his chair. Notes outstanding had a face value of $15,000,000. All this accumulation in six short months! The phone rang and interrupted his thoughts.

"Hello? Yes, hello, Captain Brady. Do you have good news for me? You've decided to take the job? Wonderful! See you in my office Monday morning." Ponzi hung up the phone with a smirk.

"A police captain wants to be one of my agents... well, I'll be damned!"

With a light tap on the door, his secretary peeked in. "Mr. Ponzi, you have a board meeting at Hanover Trust at one o'clock."

"Thank you, Lucy. Did you get the paper for me this morning?"

"Yes, sir, I'll bring it in for you." She returned and placed it on the desk and left the room. Ponzi scanned the front page. For weeks the *Boston Post* had been suspicious and had carried on a crusade against him. Richard Grozier, the assistant publisher, was hinting of investigations into the workings of the Security Exchange, but had made little headway. Grozier was certain thousands of people were headed for financial ruin—that no one could operate a business legally and pay investors so high a rate of interest. Ponzi glanced at his watch and noted it was eleven o'clock. At the same time, Lucy opened the door and announced the reporters had arrived.

"Show them in, please."

The members of the press strode in and quickly took a seat.

"Gentlemen, as you probably know, both the Postal Department and the Police Department have given my company a clean bill of health. Today, Captain Brady has notified me of his resignation from the police department and his decision to join my firm as an agent." There was a burst of exclamation by the reporters. Ponzi smiled and lit a cigar. "By the way, have any of you tried the Ponzi Cigar? It's sort of a domestic cigar with an imported name." The group laughed as they stood and left the room, anxious to report their findings. Ponzi picked up the telephone and asked the operator to connect him with his home in Lexington.

"Hello, Rose!"

"Charlie, is everything alright?"

"Of course, everything is fine. How is Mama?"

"Oh, she's very excited. We are going out for lunch and then we are going shopping for new dresses for the Mayor's Banquet tonight."

"I almost forgot about that! I have a one o'clock board meeting at Hanover, but I'll be home about the usual time. Kiss Mama for me and I'll see you both later." He hung up the phone, and, after reviewing some records, glanced at his watch.

Twelve noon, he thought. *I have just enough time to have a fast lunch and get to Hanover in time for the meeting.* He stood up and put on his suit coat. After lighting another cigar, he placed his ever-present straw hat jauntily on his head, reached for his cane, and straightened his tie. He was ready for the world.

Following the meeting, he returned to the office and found everything running smoothly. All the bushel-baskets were brimming with money. Some were so overfilled their contents spilled out onto the floor.

"Tom, pick up the overflow, will you?"

Tom turned from his customer. "Mr. Ponzi, I'll have to do it later. This customer is waiting for his receipt. He claims he was waiting in line out on the street for four hours!"

"Alright, I'll take care of it."

Ponzi stooped down and began gathering the bills scattered around the floor.

"Charlie, maybe you would like to borrow my broom?" a voice called from the line of investors. Charlie turned to find Mrs. Luigi Casullo smiling at him.

"Mrs. Casullo, how are things at the store? Tell Luigi I said hello."

"I will, Charlie. And'a how is Rose?"

"Oh, she and Mama are fine. They are getting ready to attend the Mayor's Banquet."

"How nice. Tell them to stop and visit me sometime."

"You bet, I certainly will. Take care of yourself."

After putting in a full day at the office, Ponzi decided to leave for home.

"Tom, I'm going to the Mayor's Banquet tonight, so I may be a little late tomorrow."

"No problem, Mr. Ponzi. Have a good time," Tom shouted back. Charlie hurried home to dress for the affair. In their bedroom, Rose sat at her vanity brushing her hair. Her new diamond earrings, a gift from Charlie, sparkled brilliantly as each stroke of the brush wound its way through her silky, coal black hair.

"I love my new earrings," she called out.

Charlie popped his head out of the bathroom. "Your beauty puts them to shame, my darling."

"*Bello*," she answered, fluttering her eyes.

"*Civetta*," he shot back.

She jumped from her chair and ran giggling to him. They embraced in a long kiss.

"You look beautiful, Rose."

"Do you like my gown? It's made of famous Skinner satin, manufactured in Holyoke. The lady at the dress shop said I looked stunning in red."

"She was right—you do. You are going to be the belle of the ball!"

The couple continued dressing, and soon, together with Mama, were riding to the festivities in the limousine. Ponzi entered the banquet room with Mama on one arm and Rose on the other. All eyes were on them as they approached the Mayor and his wife. Charlie loved all the attention he was receiving. He and his family were looked upon as royalty, he thought... and rightfully so!

"Good evening, Mr. Mayor. Thank you for inviting us to this wonderful banquet." Charlie extended his hand as the two Mrs. Ponzis grandly curtsied.

"Mr. Ponzi, it's very nice to have you and your family here. I hope you enjoy the evening."

"I'm sure we will," Charlie answered in earnest. The three made their way to their table. Already seated there was the Chief of Police as well as his wife and mother-in-law. Rose instantly recognized them from photos she had seen on the society page of the *Post*. Charlie sat Mama next to the Chief's mother-in-law and initiated the introductions.

The group chatted happily and enjoyed the sumptuous dinner. In between the seven courses,

Charlie swept Rose around the dance floor, to the glances and smiles of all the onlookers. Later, as everyone at the table sipped their wine, the police chief leaned forward. "Mr. Ponzi, thanks to you, many of our officers have found themselves with a bounty of overtime. It's all I can do to keep the traffic flowing smoothly around School Street. It's quite a business you have going there!"

"I'm sorry about the congestion and the traffic snarls," Ponzi apologized profusely. "We try to keep things in an orderly fashion, but, when dealing with such masses, it is difficult."

"Oh, please don't apologize. This is the most excitement Boston has had in a long time. Besides, it keeps the men in my department on their toes. Isn't that right, Mr. Mayor?"

The Mayor nodded. "Yes, it's hard to believe you've created such a stir in so short a time, Mr. Ponzi."

"I understand you are an active member of the board at Hanover," said the chief. "Is that true?"

"Yes, it appears our city's fathers have deemed it fit to appoint me to a decision-making position," replied Ponzi. "I derive great satisfaction in the knowledge of, as well as the participation in, Boston's banking system."

"Yes, well, you are certainly getting your experience handling money," the chief admitted with a laugh.

Charlie gave a secret wink to Rose and turned back to him. "And, by any chance, have *you* invested in my company?"

"As a matter of fact, I did invest a small amount last month. And, by the way...got my money returned along with fifty per cent interest."

"Excellent! I do like to hear from my satisfied customers," Charlie crowed. Rose whispered in Ponzi's ear. "Charlie, Mama looks a bit tired." She leaned over to her. "Are you all right, Mama?"

"Well, it has been a long day…"

"Then we should say our goodbyes and leave. We don't want you to overdo it."

"It looks as though your son is taking very good care of you, Mrs. Ponzi," observed the mayor.

"Your honor, my son Charlie is… *meraviglioso*!"

"And what does that mean, Mrs. Ponzi?"

"It means…wonderful!" the elderly Mrs. Ponzi answered with immense pride.

Chapter 15

Ponzi gazed upon the score of newspapers scattered over his desk. He began to read the numerous stories and profiles written about himself and his meteoric rise to power. *The Rochester Times-Union* was the first he picked up, and it said, "Only a few months ago he was a dishwasher. A man untaught in finance shows Wall Street and the greatest financiers in the world that they are pikers." The word brought him much amusement. "Whether Ponzi's bubble bursts or not, the American people will have to take off their hats to a man as clever as he is." *The Knickerbocker Press* stated, "Ponzi's scheme is simplicity itself. He has exposed it all voluntarily, to the much-exercised state and national officials—with the exception of the trifling detail of how he works it."

The Boston News Bureau was not as flattering, however. With financial expert C.W. Barron as its publisher, the *Bureau* pooh-poohed Ponzi's whole scheme under the headline, "Why Not Stop The Farce?" Fuming, Charlie called in his secretary.

"Lucy, call my attorney and tell him I plan to sue Mr. Barron of the *Boston News Bureau* in the amount of $5,000,000 for libel. Notify the press of my plans and tell them they can quote me as follows: "I have forgotten more about international finance than Barron ever knew."

"Yes, sir. Right away."

Pleased with his planned response to Barron, Ponzi picked up the *New York Evening World* and settled back to enjoy its colorful report.

"All of Boston is get-rich-quick mad over Charles Ponzi, the creator of fortunes, a modern King Midas, who doubles your money in ninety days. At every corner, on the street-cars, behind the department-store counters, from luxurious parlor to humble kitchen, to the very outskirts of New England, Ponzi is making more hope, more anxiety, than any conquering general of old. Mary Pickford, Sir Thomas Lipton, and smuggling booze over the Canadian border aren't in it anymore. For Ponzi makes everybody rich quick. Loan him your money, from fifty dollars to fifty thousand dollars, and in ninety days he gives you back twice as much as you gave him. He's been going at it for eight months and he's still at it."

And I'll keep at it as long as I can, thought Ponzi smugly.

"With no other security than his personal note, Boston is pouring its savings into Ponzi's hands. Like a tidal wave, the passion for investment sees them selling their Liberty bonds and getting money from loan sharks in order to get in on the get-rich-quick proposition. Police officials are said to be heavy investors. 'It must be all right if District Attorney Pelletier invested twenty-five thousand dollars,' remarked one stately woman dressed in the height of fashion."

Pelletier, thought Ponzi. *I thought he was investigating me! Hmm, I'll have to send a note of thanks to the D.A. for the vote of confidence.*

"There's never been anything like it before in Boston, they say, and no one knows where it will end. When questioned in conference with Daniel J.

Gallagher, United States Attorney, Ponzi said also that he had in the United States upward of $5,000,000 and between $8,000,000 and $9,000,000 in depositories abroad."

"'This enterprise is just preliminary to something much bigger,' Ponzi says. He adds he is going to start a worldwide banking system whereby net profits would be divided equally between the stockholders and the depositors."

"Postal inspectors who are working with United States Attorney Daniel Gallagher on the case are unable to discover where Ponzi obtained the many millions of stamps necessary to carry on his business. Investigations are being made here and abroad, but as of yet Ponzi's secret has not been revealed. He continues to pay his debts, and faith in him multiplies as each note-bearer emerges with a smile, and with twice as much cash in his hands as he put in two months before. Payment is being made to all comers over a hastily improvised cashier's counter in his office. Ponzi opened an office in the "Bell-in Hand" to meet the demands upon him growing out of newspaper notoriety he attained when the method by which he made his quick fortune became known, and today he said that during the first day there, was paid out over the counter hundreds of thousands of dollars. He declared he could put $5,000,000 on the table at any time and that every obligation would be met."

"The new Italian banker has swept over Boston folk until it took half of Boston's police force to subdue the enthusiasm of a throng of prospective investors that overflow from the banking office, through corridors, down the stairs, and onto the streets, blocking traffic. So tremendous has been the withdrawal of funds from savings banks that it is rumored there is consternation in high financial circles."

"Trading in international coupons, taking advantage of the various rates of exchange with foreign countries in peculiar combination, Ponzi says, enables him to coin fortunes for himself and everyone who invests with him. Federal, State, and local investigation has failed to unearth anything illegitimate about the business. Police officials and district attorneys are said to be heavy investors. 'The biggest skeptics are now my biggest believers,' says Ponzi. Estimates are made that more than half a million persons have invested, every note has been paid at maturity with fifty per cent, interest in forty-five days, one hundred percent in ninety days. Notes are redeemed at face value at any time."

"In a dingy little office, on one of Boston's busy streets, close by the old Revolutionary burying grounds, Ponzi, meteoric banker, doles out his notes and takes in the money. In narrow corridors, up the stairways, at the doorways, with the air hot and dense from the crowds who have gathered day by day, handsome women with jewels, in their ears and the money-mad fever in their eyes, touch unkempt women with babies in their arms and children tagging at their skirts."

"There's a terrible tenseness in the air and excitement runs high, the hands of big men are trembling and some women stutter as they talk. Lifetime savings are given away as if under the touch of an unseen hypnotist. Gaunt old maids give their money away as if it were pest-ridden, boys in knickerbockers gladly turn over all their wealth. Widows in long black veils, stenographers, fruit-peddlers in their overalls, all kinds, young and old, rich and poor, some looking affluent, some downtrodden, jostle and push and sometimes fight to get a place nearer the magic entrance."

"Ponzi's promptness in providing measures to meet all proper demands has so impressed the Equity Session of the Superior Court that Judge Waite refused an application by David Stoneman, counsel for Alton Parker of Boston for the appointment of a temporary receiver for Ponzi's funds. A rival concern started across the hall fails to draw supporters from the Ponzi get-rich-quick establishment. To 'Charles Ponzi, head of the Securities Exchange Company' points a large sign on the first floor of the building, and that is where they all go."

And right they should, thought Ponzi. *No one can match me!*

A knock at the door interrupted his thoughts. Lucy entered the room.

"Sir, the reporter from the *New York Times* has arrived for his appointment."

Ponzi quickly picked up the pile of newspapers he had been enjoying off of his desk and threw them in the basket.

"Send him in."

A distinguished-looking elderly man in a gray pinstripe suit walked in with pen and pad. "Hello, Mr. Ponzi. I'm from the *Times*."

Ponzi shook his extended hand. "I'm delighted to make your acquaintance. It will be my pleasure to speak with you today, but, as I'm on a very tight schedule, we will have to limit our interview to fifteen minutes. I must join my wife and mother for dinner."

"But, sir, I've traveled a very long distance to meet with you. That is hardly enough time to speak with the man who is the topic of conversation wherever you turn in New England."

Ponzi smiled, but ignored the flattery. "That's very clever of you. I have been reading your accounts of my success in the *Times*. I am aware that you are the Boston correspondent for the newspaper. That means you live here in the area. You are welcome to schedule a second appointment with my secretary."

He offered a chair to the reporter. The correspondent sat down clearing his throat slightly and a bit awkwardly, realizing his foolishness at underestimating his subject. Ponzi went over to the hastily set up bar and picked up a bottle and two glasses. "Can I offer you a Campari and one of my namesake cigars?"

"No, thank you, I like to write with a clear head." He quietly opened his pad and began scribbling as he spoke. "Your success, sir, in spite of great obstacles, confounds your critics. Our readers are very interested in any fiduciary advice you may have to offer. To start, I would like to inquire as to your upbringing and personal background."

Ponzi lit a cigar. "My family was well-to-do in Italy; my education was of the best. We had considerable money, but were not extremely wealthy. However, we had plenty. I never had to do any work of any kind and felt that it was beneath me in my own country to engage in labor of any kind, so I kept at school in Parma, Italy, and then went into the University of Rome.

"I'll be very frank with you," Ponzi went on. "In my college days I was what you call over here a 'spendthrift.' That is, I had arrived at that precarious period in a young man's life when spending money seemed the most attractive thing on earth."

"Ah, yes," the correspondent replied. "I remember my own like phase."

"Do you? Well, then, you know that such a game is like a balloon—it goes up all right, but sooner or later it has got to come down." They both chuckled at the image. "To make a long story short, I felt that I must get to work, and not wanting to do so with all my acquaintances about me, I decided to come to America. I did not have much money then, and came to this country—right here to Boston—just like any immigrant. And when I arrived, my total wealth was just $2.50."

The reporter's eyebrows raised in surprise. Ponzi leaned back, loosened his tie, and continued to reflect on those hard times.

"As I say, I landed in this country with $2.50 in cash and one million dollars in hopes, and those hopes never left me. I was always dreaming of the day I could get enough money on which I could make more money, because it is a cinch no man is going to make money unless he has got money to start on. I saved a bit of money from off jobs and felt like having a good time, so I went to Coney Island and had the time of my life for a couple of weeks. Then my cash was gone. So into the big town of New York I went to find a job."

"And what did you work at?"

"Up at one of the big hotels they needed some waiters, and they even furnished me with the tuxedo service coat. Yep, I've carried tons of food, and with the small salary and tips I made enough to live. I went from one waiting job to another; worked in various hotels, small restaurants, and did my dishwashing stint, from necessity at times. I got tired of New York and began to travel, getting jobs all along the way. Once, when I was in Florida, I got it into my head that I could make something painting signs, so I bought some cardboard and paint and started it. No, I never had the slightest experience, but I got away with it, satisfied folks, and made a little cash. And all the time I kept dreaming of the time I was going to do big things."

"It sounds to me like the modest beginnings of a budding entrepreneur—and a well-traveled one at that," observed the reporter.

"Yes," agreed Ponzi. "It was small jobs and more small jobs up to the year 1917, when I headed for Boston once more, saw an advertisement in a Boston paper, answered it, and took a job with J.R. Poole, a merchandise broker. My salary was twenty-five dollars a week."

"I see. So the seeds of your success were sown from the ground floor of an investment company."

Ponzi marveled at how newspapermen came to their own conclusions. "And then I found my inspiration. She was Rose Gnecco, daughter of a wholesale fruit merchant of Boston, and the fairest and most wonderful woman in the world."

"I have seen a photo of her. She is indeed quite beautiful," the reporter agreed.

"All I have done is because of Rose. She is not only my right arm, but my heart, as well. We were married in February, 1918."

"But may we continue speaking about your business interests? Would you agree that you might possibly owe your current financial opportunity to the reactions of the World War?"

"Absolutely," Ponzi replied. "This business of mine can be only temporary at best, simply while the foreign exchange conditions remain as they are. The minute the exchange offers no margin, then this business stops."

"Then you will retire for life on your twelve million dollars?" queried his interviewer.

"I will not," Ponzi answered with emphasis. "I will just begin to do my life-work. You know, this whole fracas at present is due to just one state of affairs. Bankers and businessmen can easily understand how I could make one hundred per cent for myself, but simply because no one ever made an added fifty per cent for the general public, they reason that it can't be. You remember the old Rube who saw the giraffe for the first time? He stared at it and remarked, 'There ain't no such animal.' The truth is, bankers and businessmen have been doing plenty for themselves under the present banking system, but they have done little for anybody else. I want to change this unfair condition. The depositor in the banks today is not getting a square deal. I shall endeavor to create an institution where the depositor will get what he ought to get, even if it does shake up the old crowd."

"How will this institution be organized, and who will be responsible for its solvency?"

"To be sure, the stockholders assume responsibility, and this should be taken into account. Therefore, I believe the stockholders should receive a certain designated per cent, to cover this responsibility, and that the depositors get their regular rate of interest, but on top of this I believe that the extra earnings, instead of it all going to the stockholders, would be divided fifty-fifty between stockholders and depositors."

The reporter raised an eyebrow again as he continued scribbling.

"Yes, I know it is a shock to some of these folks who have been hogging it all, but it is fair and right, and the depositor should get a fair return for his money," explained Ponzi.

His secretary interrupted any further remarks. "Excuse me, sir, but Mr. McMasters is here and would like to speak with you."

Ponzi was surprised at the unexpected visit. "Tell him I'll be with him in a moment." He turned back to the reporter. "McMasters is helping me with publicity."

"One last question, Mr. Ponzi: I've noted with great interest an advertisement in our latest editions from a savings bank nearby. They point to your current achievements and are offering five and a quarter percent. Do you have any comment?"

"A pathetic and futile attempt to garner some of my investors, no doubt." Ponzi smiled and shook his hand. "My best wishes to you. Thank you for writing about me and my business."

"Not at all. I am merely doing a service for the public to let them know about you. I will be following this story closely and will speak with you again very soon."

The correspondent left the office. McMasters stormed in a few minutes later.

"Ah, Larry, what brings you here today?"

McMasters came straight to the front of the desk and confronted Ponzi. "Charles, I don't know quite how to say this, but I don't believe I can work for you anymore!"

Ponzi stubbed out his cigar. "Now, don't get excited, Larry. Sit down and tell me what is wrong. I'm sure we can discuss this like gentlemen and solve the problem."

"You don't understand the ways of the publicity world, Charles! I've been trying to be your liaison with the media and you consistently set up appointments with them behind my back! All anyone has to do is call on you for a comment and you sing like a bird. Lucy said that today you were talking with a man from the *Times*! All requests for interviews with you must be cleared through me—that is what you hired me for, remember?"

"Well, Larry, I'm awfully sorry if I hurt your feelings. But may I remind you that I was doing fine before you came along, and you'll just have to understand that if I feel like granting an interview on the spur of the moment, I will. The public wants to be kept aware of what I'm thinking and doing."

McMasters leaned in over the desk. "Charles, that's what concerns me. So many people look up to you now. They hang on to every word you speak. They'd follow you anywhere. They'd do anything you tell them to do, including investing their life savings with you. Do you realize how much power you're wielding? You're in danger of abusing that power, as well as the trust the public has placed in you. When I first met you, I thought you were a visionary. I thought your ideas were going to be able to make all of those dreams every poor, little guy has come true. I hoped I'd be able to help you expand your ideas nationally and eventually globally. But the frightening part is that you don't have any real plan. You *never* had one. This whole thing is just a scam! And I can't continue to be a part of it."

Ponzi swallowed hard. "Larry, you don't know what you're saying. I have a plan, I really do. I just need some time to work it all out. You can help me with it, I know you can."

"No, I'm sorry, I can't." He began to exit the office, but stopped short of the door and turned. "You know, eventually, your withdrawals will outnumber your deposits. You won't be able to make good on your promises. Everyone will want answers. The rats won't follow the Pied Piper forever." He left the room.

Ponzi mulled over the situation, trying to forget McMasters's words of impending doom.

Chapter 16

After working for Ponzi for only a few short months, McMasters had become disillusioned with his employer. Ponzi had ceased being a hero to the publicist. McMasters felt his visit to Ponzi served as an effective resignation. He took a short walk to the *Post* and asked for Richard Grozier.

"I have a great story, and I'd be happy to write it for you," McMasters declared.

"Well, that's very interesting. Please sit down," replied Grozier. "What is the basis for this disclosure?"

"Let's just say that I think it's about time to call a halt to Charles Ponzi and show him for the swindler he really is. Ponzi is hopelessly insolvent. I've estimated that he's in debt to the tune of between two and four million dollars, and that figure continues to grow every day. In short, he's crooked...as crooked as a winding staircase! And I've got the goods on him."

"You write that story, and I'll give it recognition. In fact, we'll publish it in a special edition!" Grozier found it hard to contain his excitement.

McMasters sat down at his typewriter and started hammering out his charges against Ponzi for the *Boston Post*. Grozier read the finished product and was completely delighted.

"It's great, just great! Let's see Ponzi survive the run on his company after the public gets a load of this stuff," he said, smiling broadly.

McMasters's article appeared on the front page of the *Post* on the second of August. The story started another and more serious run on the Security Exchange office. A bobbing mass of straw hats again covered School Street. Ponzi supporters passed out handbills defending him and his company and chastising the publishers and bankers who were constantly attacking him. Even then, the little investors were still keeping faith in their hero. He was the courageous man who dared to stand up to the bankers and win at their own game. Speculators walked up and down the lines of those investors, waiting to get their payoff, and offered to buy the notes at a reduced rate. Ponzi made a surprise appearance.

"Ladies and gentlemen, I assure you, you have nothing to fear," he shouted to the crowd in the street. "If you are here to cash in your notes, you will be giving up certain profits!" He smiled confidently, waved his cane to the throng of people, and entered the stairway to his office. That day Ponzi handed out hundreds of thousands of dollars, and kept his followers with him. The money still came in and overflowed the bushel baskets behind the teller's cages. He paid his notes with checks from the Hanover Trust Company, to which he now owed a quarter of a million dollars. Later that day Ponzi walked to the courthouse to file a five million dollar suit against the *Post*. As he passed the newspaper building, he thumbed his nose at it and those supporters walking with him cheered. Ponzi was still the poor-man's Midas, but dark clouds were gathering.

That same day, Joe Allen sat patiently waiting for his meeting with the governor. The secretary stepped into the inner office and soon appeared, signaling Allen to follow. He entered the larger office and walked to the desk.

"Good day, Governor Coolidge. Good to see you again, sir."

"Commissioner Allen, it's nice to see you as well." He gestured to a chair before the desk.

"I got your message and came as soon as I could," Allen said, quickly taking a seat.

"Commissioner, it seems we have a serious problem on our hands, and it is urgent that we find an immediate remedy. Mr. Ponzi has caused us considerable concern, and he is slowly undermining the essence of our entire banking system. We need positive action. Do you have any suggestions?"

"Yes. And I hope this meets with your approval. I have decided to close the Hanover Trust. To the public, it may seem like an extreme measure; however, since Ponzi is a board member of that bank, and uses that location for his bank transactions, we need to freeze his assets. If his company is indeed solvent, as he claims, he will have no problems continuing business as usual."

"I think, under the circumstances, we should institute this procedure immediately. I have confidence in your ability to handle this situation," Coolidge declared.

Joe smiled modestly, relieved that his theory had received such a warm reception. "Thank you, Governor, but you are aware of the possibility that we may lose that bank if any discrepancies are discovered."

"If we do, so be it! Better to lose one bank than to jeopardize them all. Would you like a cup of coffee,

Commissioner?" the governor asked as he rang for his secretary.

"Yes, thank you."

"Miss Moore, bring in some coffee, please."

Joe and Governor Coolidge relaxed as the woman carried in a tray. She poured coffee and handed a cup to both men. As soon as she left the room Coolidge resumed the conversation. "This thing has all the earmarks of a frighteningly enormous hoax. I hope we can bring the situation to a halt before more innocent victims are duped!"

"I agree. I understand that Ponzi now has several agents in his employ as far away as Rhode Island. His racket has spread to western Massachusetts as well as Connecticut."

"What is the first step you'll be taking?" questioned the governor.

"I will draw up the necessary papers, and after you sign them, I will deliver them personally to the bank, where there will be an immediate takeover and closing. Since Ponzi is using Hanover Trust checks to pay off his investors, it should throw a serious wrench into his future business transactions!"

The governor stood and extended his hand, offering a firm handshake.

"Commissioner, it's been good talking with you. I'll be awaiting those papers. Good day."

Allen picked up his hat. "Good day to you, sir."

At about the same time, a group of men sat around the table in another large, private office. A short, stocky man puffed on a cigar while a lanky, dark-complexioned one doodled on a pad. A blanket of silence covered the room as they all patiently waited. The door suddenly opened, and the boss entered, quickly striding to his seat at the head of the table. Clearing his throat, he broke the silence.

"We all know why we're here. Rumor has it that the new bank commissioner has decided to investigate Ponzi. We're not goin' to tolerate this. What's to stop the Feds from zeroing in on *us*, after they put the heat on Ponzi? I think it's time to nip this thing in the bud!" Grunts of approval sounded throughout the room.

"I say we put a contract out on Allen. I'll give one of you boys the job. And after it's done he'll take a little vacation out of the country until the heat's off... Any problems with that?" growled the man in charge.

Nobody spoke out against the idea.

"OK, then, it's settled." He looked over at one man. "You get the job, Rocky. Come back tonight, got it?"

"Sure, boss, no problem."

"Now, the other matter on the agenda. That shopkeeper on View Street...I think he needs a visit from Fingers and Aldo. You know, to help persuade him to be a little more cooperative. Just pay him a little visit and show him we mean business." He banged the table violently for emphasis. "We're not puttin' up with his shit any longer! He either coughs up like the others or he's history. Alright, boys, that's it!"

The men rose from the table and began to line up. The boss held Rocky back for a moment. "Rocky, after you take care of Allen, I want you to go to the old country. Hey...you can visit all your cousins, right?"

"That's great with me, boss. I'd love to see my cousin Gina!"

"Yeah, we've all heard about your cousin Gina..." He cleared his throat. "Just don't forget to come back!"

The group of men shook the boss's hand and quietly left the room single file. Rocky was the last to leave.

"Rock, I'll take good care of you, I promise. This is a *big* job. Allen's pretty important in Massachusetts. You take care of him, and they'll know we mean business, right? We'll set you up with ten G's and you can relax for a while."

"Don't worry, boss, there'll be no screw-ups." Rocky placed his hat on his head and walked out the door.

The boss walked over to the window and looked down at the street. He took a big puff on his cigar. "There's only one way I want Allen," he said, glancing down in time to see a roach scurry across the floor. His foot came down on the insect with a thud. Smiling to himself, he whispered, "Dead!"

Rocky hurried to Sharkey's, ordered a drink, and downed it. The possibility of Helen's involvement with the boss ate away at his gut.

That bastard is pretty smart, he thought. *He chooses me to knock off Allen, then pays me off and ships me out! That way, he and Helen have all the time in the world to screw around while* I'm *out of the picture.* "Well...maybe Rock ain't so dumb after all," he muttered to himself. He snuffed out his cigarette and left the bar.

It was dark by the time Fingers and Aldo pulled up in front of Antonio's Butcher Shop. A dim light in the back room shone through the drawn curtains, and a tilted 'closed' sign hung on the front door. The two slowly walked down the alley to the back of the building.

A saw could be heard breaking the still of the night as Antonio worked on preparing tomorrow's choice cuts of meat. Aldo put his shoulder to the old back door and threw his weight at it with full force, causing it to cave in... and as it did, he lost his footing and stumbled into the back room.

The screeching sound of the saw grating against animal bone was deafening and kept Antonio unaware of the two intruders. The butcher felt a hand on his shoulder and he whirled around in surprise.

"What the hell are you doin' here? Whaddaya what?" Antonio demanded. He turned off the saw and faced the two burly men. Antonio was also a big man, well over two hundred fifty pounds and at least six foot four- a man to be reckoned with and confident of his strength and stature. Glaring at the two, he whipped off his apron and held up his fists.

"You're not bein' a smart boy, Antonio. You're behind in your protection payments and the boss is pretty mad," Fingers said as he lit a cigarette.

"I don't need no protection. Now get out of my shop or I'll throw you both out!" yelled the butcher, shaking with anger.

Aldo pulled out a gun and waved it in the air. "I don't think you wanna argue with this!" he snarled.

Antonio lunged at Aldo as the gun went off and fell to the floor. Fingers pulled his gun and used the butt to deliver a hard blow to the back of the butcher's head. Antonio dropped to the floor with a loud thud.

It was some time before Antonio came to. He slowly opened his eyes, shaking his head to clear it, and he realized that he was tied to a chair, with the tight rope cutting into his chest and legs. One arm was free.

"Welcome back to reality," laughed Fingers. "Tony, Tony...you don't mind me callin' you 'Tony', do you?... Aldo and me were really hopin' you'd see things our way."

Aldo came around to the side of Antonio and whispered in his ear. "But no, Tony... you hadda make it difficult."

"I never paid for protection. I don't need it," insisted the butcher.

"Sorry, friend. I beg to differ witcha," Fingers hissed as he grabbed a handful of Antonio's hair and pulled back his head. Aldo grabbed his hand and placed it on the butcher block.

"Wait a minute! Whaddaya doin'?" Antonio gasped as he struggled frantically to free his hand.

"What are we doin'? We're goin' to teach you a little lesson, you stubborn bastard!" Aldo yelled.

Fingers picked up Antonio's cleaver. The well-honed blade was stained with animal blood. "The next time we come to collect, Tony, you fuckin' better cough it up!"

The cleaver came down on the block with a sickening thump. Antonio screamed as his blood splattered everywhere, and one of his fingers rolled rapidly across the wooden block.

"You son of a bitch!!!" he exclaimed as his face contorted with searing pain.

"Look at this!" Aldo yelled at Fingers. "Now you did it, dammit! You ruined it!" he whined as he pointed to his crimson splattered tie.

"Hey, you never looked good wearin' that piece o' shit anyway," laughed Fingers.

The two looked back at Antonio who by now hung limply in the chair, unconscious from the attack.

"Untie him... he can patch himself up when he comes to," Fingers ordered as he walked out of the back room.

Chapter 17

Joe walked into Hanover Trust and asked a security guard where the president's office was located. The guard pointed to a door to the left of the lobby. Allen nodded a thank you and strode to the door. After knocking, he opened the door and saw a very anxious man seated behind the desk. Henry Chmielenski stood and quickly rounded the desk to shake hands with the commissioner.

"Commissioner Allen, welcome! Do sit down."

"How do you do, Mr. Chmielenski. What I have to say will not take long. Hanover Trust is in a very serious state of affairs. Mr. Ponzi is now indebted to this bank for over a quarter of a million dollars! This bank has shown extremely poor judgement in conducting business and granting loans. I am forced to seize and close this bank immediately."

"But, sir...isn't this a rather radical action you're taking? Surely with a little time we can alter...perhaps... rectify the situation," he stammered.

"I'm sorry, but it's too late for a quick fix," Joe admonished the man sternly. "It is imperative that action be taken right now."

A large group gathered outside the doors of the bank as Joe posted signs and made an official statement.

"Under the authority vested in me, by law, I hereby take possession of the property and business of the Hanover Trust Company," he announced to a stunned crowd.

"Why are you taking this action?" shouted a reporter.

"I have decided to close Hanover Trust because our department has been investigating Hanover since last week and has found it to be doing business in an unsafe manner. This bank has violated the law in loaning $500,000 to Mr. Ponzi on his certificate of deposit for $1,500,000, thereby constituting a withdrawal of the deposit before the time specified. The general condition of this bank's loans is unsatisfactory. Many loans were found to be excessive, some are beyond the legal limit, and many are of doubtful value!"

"Do you think this bank is insolvent?" the reporter probed further.

"I fear its capital has been impaired," Allen answered.

The bank was immediately shut down and the employees dismissed, with Allen leaving behind a mob of angry customers wanting to make withdrawals.

Later that day, the phone rang in Allen's office. The secretary stepped into the room. "Commissioner Allen, it's a call for you."

"Who is it? If it's a reporter, tell him I'll have an official statement at four o'clock."

"I don't think it's a reporter, sir. He just said he had some important information."

The secretary left as Allen picked up the receiver. "Hello, this is Commissioner Allen speaking..."

"Allen? You're going to be a dead man when you least expect it!"

Joe looked at the receiver with shock as the phone line went dead. He immediately dialed home. "Hart, is everything all right?"

"Yes, everything is fine, Joe. Why do you ask? What's wrong?"

"Hart, I want you to stay indoors today. Do you understand?"

"Yes, of course, dear...but why?"

"I think we may be in great danger..."

"Oh my God..."

"I'll explain when I get home tonight."

"All right, dear," Hart answered with a tremor in her voice.

Joe immediately called the Governor's office. "Governor, I just received a threatening phone call. There may be a contract out on my life."

"I was afraid something like that might happen," was the reply. "The state will be happy to provide an armed guard for your protection for as long as necessary. We can't fool around with these characters."

"Thank you, sir. I think I'll need it. And you're right, I wouldn't put anything past them!"

"I'll send someone immediately. Do be careful... if there is anything else I can do, don't hesitate to call!"

"Thank you, Governor, I'll do that. Good day."

Allen hung up the phone and stood in the silent room wondering what was to become of him and his wife. He felt like a passenger on a runaway train, totally out of control with no idea of its destination. At four o'clock, the outer office was filled to capacity with members of the press. Allen stepped out under the watchful eyes of state troopers and cleared his throat, waiting for a hush to fall over the room.

"Gentlemen...as you know, at one forty-five p.m. today I took possession of and closed the Hanover Trust. After a thorough investigation, I have found that the bank has been operating in an unprofessional and illegal manner."

"Are you investigating a possible closing of other banks?" shouted a reporter from the back of the room.

"I have no further information to give out at this time. Thank you, gentlemen, and good day."

There was a burst of questions and comments as Joe turned, entered his office, and closed the door behind him. He felt obliged to withhold any further information until the probe was complete and all the reports were in his hands.

Promptly at five o'clock, Joe picked up his briefcase and left the office with the guard at his side. Together they caught the train to Newton Highlands and silently sat through the entire ride home. Joe's mind was racing like the wheels on the train. The monotonous sound made his head ache, and his stomach churned with thoughts of the death threat that had been thrust upon him. The train pulled into the station and the two men stepped out and surveyed the empty platform. With his briefcase under his arm, Joe and his attendant began the walk home, staying in the center of the road for the entire two blocks. The sidewalks were heavily lined with thick bushes, therefore the guard felt the road would be much safer. Once in front of his house, Joe thanked the guard.

"No problem, sir. Rest assured we will keep you and your wife under surveillance at all times, Mr. Allen. You will be perfectly safe," he assured the nervous commissioner.

Joe quickly entered the house and bolted the door.
"Hart, where are you?"
"I'm in the kitchen..."
"We are going to have to take precautions..."

"Precautions?"

"Yes. For starters, I don't want you to leave the screened windows open. From now on, open the windows from the top instead..."

"But why? What's going on?"

"Now don't get excited, Hart, but there's been a threat on my life..."

"Oh, my God, Joe! What are we going to do?"

"We will just go about our business and exercise extreme caution. I want you to be sure all the doors are always kept locked. Don't open them unless you know the caller."

"What about you? How are you going to protect yourself? What about Sunday? Mother and Father are coming for dinner! Should I cancel?"

"No, we will go on with our plans—we'll just keep our eyes open. This could just be an idle threat, but we don't want to take any chances."

"Is the governor aware of all this?"

"Yes, I called and told him. He offered protection, and I accepted. The state police will shadow us. But I don't want this situation to become conspicuous. This could be the prank of some disgruntled Hanover customer."

"Let's hope so!" Hart said as she shook her head.

On Sunday, Hart tried her best to be as cheerful as possible, for her parent's sake. Mother saw right through the charade.

"Hart, you're not yourself today. You're acting happy, but I sense there is something bothering you."

Hart whispered, "I'll tell you, Mother, but it must be held in the strictest of confidence."

"Well, of course, dear."

"Someone called Joe and threatened his life."

Mother's eyes widened. "Heavens, no wonder you're upset! Did you report it to the authorities?"

Hart nodded. "Joe doesn't want it to become public, but he did tell the governor. We now have armed escorts and state police watching out for us. Mother, I'm so afraid for him—I'm beside myself!"

"Hart...whatever the two of you decide to do, please be careful!"

"Please don't tell Father or the family. The fewer that know, the better."

"Yes, dear, I understand."

At dinner the four discussed various topics. Father questioned Joe about the closing of Hanover, at which time Hart dropped her fork and excused her clumsiness.

"William, let's not discuss business. You can get all the facts in the Evening News," Mother interrupted.

"Yes, well, we all know how factual the newspapers can be..." Father added in a huff.

"Let's move to the living room for a sherry, shall we?" Hart suggested.

"Good idea!" Joe added.

"Isn't it a bit early to have the curtains drawn?" Father questioned, settling into an overstuffed chair.

"William, perhaps Hart and Joe enjoy their privacy."

"Yes, well...privacy is good," Father agreed, looking rather confused.

"Joe, please fill the glasses and pass them around," said Hart, who was happy with Mother's attempt at running interference for her.

Before too long, Joseph the chauffeur could be heard pulling into the driveway. Hart hugged her parents. "Come again soon, darlings, it was wonderful having you visit."

"It was a treat seeing you, Hart." Father gave her a big hug. "Next time, you come visit us. It will give our cook an excuse to make one of her big fancy cakes."

Mother and Father left and Hart closed the door, leaning against it with a huge sigh of relief. "I can't wait until this is all over," she confessed.

"It won't be over for some time. I've been examining the books of four other banks. I'm bound to make a lot of enemies!"

"This is such a nightmare... How did this happen in so short a time?" Hart asked.

"A few greedy people, led by someone who will probably go down in history as America's greatest swindler!"

The couple retired early, but Joe lay staring at the wall. Sleep would not come, as his mind filled with events of the past week. *There is no way I will come out of this unscathed*, he thought. *Those believing in Ponzi will be hard to convince... I'll be the logical person to blame for everyone's losses.* Worst of all, things were far from a quick fix stage. *Hanover is just the tip of the giant iceberg, an iceberg that could be as devastating and deadly as the one that hit the Titanic*, he thought. *I'll have to check out the Cosmopolitan, Fidelity, and maybe even the Tremont before I can give the system a clean bill of health. Damn, this has turned into one hell-of-a-nightmare*, he decided, shaking his head in disbelief as he tossed and turned.

Chapter 18

Rocky waited in the storage room near Allen's office. The boss told him Allen left work every day at five o'clock sharp. Right on time, Allen stepped out of his office and walked down the hall and entered the elevator. Rocky ducked out of the storage room and jumped into the elevator to join him.

"You know, bank commissioners should watch who they take elevator rides with..."

Joe looked at Rocky and asked hoarsely, "Who are you and what do you want?" Joe's stomach was taking a fast ride to the first floor, and the elevator wasn't even moving.

"It doesn't matter *who* I am. I want to talk with you."

"What would you and I have to talk about?"

"Let me put it this way: I coulda' dropped you as soon as you stepped out into the hall, but I decided to be a nice guy. In fact...I got some information you might be interested in."

Allen slowly looked into the stranger's eyes. "My guard is waiting for me in the lobby."

Rocky gestured with his hand. "There's a little diner across the street. It's public enough for you to feel safe. Meet me there...you'll be glad you did."

Allen nodded slowly as the stranger got off on the second floor, and Allen continued his ride down to the lobby. He exited the building, paused, and turned to the guard. "I'm going to catch dinner at the diner across the street. I'll only be about twenty minutes."

"No problem, sir... I'll wait outside for you."

Joe walked in and saw Rocky was waiting at a corner table, somewhat hidden by a potted plant. Joe's eyes narrowed to thin slits. "Look, I don't know who you are, but you'd better state your business quickly. My guard will be in to check on me if I'm not out in a few minutes."

Rocky smiled. "Guard, huh? Well, buddy, you're a *lot* smarter than my boss thinks you are." He leaned in and his tone of voice changed. "This won't take long. You know, personally, I can't stand any of you investigators, let alone *meet* one of you for a cup o' Joe... If my boss wasn't screwin' that goddamn whore of mine you'd be gone in a matter of days. Your remains would be *in* a cup...Joe. It just happens to be your lucky day."

Allen looked at Rocky blankly. "I don't appreciate your threats."

"Oh, you're really scarin' me. All *you* need to know is that a contract's been put out on your life, and I'm the guy who was supposed to do the job."

Joe sat back, stunned. Questions flashed through his mind. "Why are you telling me this? Why would you want to help me?" he asked softly.

"For several reasons. Something smells fishy with this Ponzi guy. Not like I feel a need to help you guys bring him down, but I do have some friends who are gonna go under if Ponzi don't pay what he owes 'em. My boss is a big fan of his, and that's why he wants you out of the way. But the most important reason is that I'm gonna get back at that two-faced bitch and screw over the boss at the same time. You know, it'll be like killing two birds with one stone." He chuckled. "Sorry, bad joke. I'm taking the money and running. I got friends over in Europe that nobody even knows about. But here's *my* advice to you: get some protection from Coolidge 'cause when I don't plug you they're gonna assign somebody else to do it. Or maybe it'll be one of those investors out in the street. They're gonna want your ass in a sling once you shut Ponzi down for good."

Allen was lost in thought about his good fortune in finding out about the contract.

Rocky stood up to leave. "Now go home to your little wife."

Allen looked at him thankfully. "I owe you my life. If you need safe transit I could help arrange it..."

Rocky smirked as he put his coat on. "Oh, yeah, sure. Thanks, anyway... I don't need a sign on me that says 'stool pigeon.' I may be crazy, pal, but I'm not stupid."

Rocky left the diner and drove back to the boss's office. After climbing the long staircase, he rapped loudly on the door and entered the room. The boss wheeled around from behind his desk. He stood and handed Rocky an envelope.

"Here's your ten G's. As soon as you finish the job, take off right away. Just be sure...no mistakes!"

"You got it." Rocky reached for the envelope. "Don't worry, everything's under control!" He turned and left the room with a grin on his face.

He went back to Sharkey's for a quick drink and to take care of some unfinished business. *That Allen's a lucky sonofabitch, that I'm his triggerman*, he thought to himself as he sat on a stool at the end of the bar. *And right now, he could be gettin' his head blown off! Instead, he's gonna go on livin' and bein' a pain in the ass to the mob and Ponzi. And me...I'm goin' on a nice trip, compliments of the boss*! He snickered silently to himself and patted the envelope filled with bills in his breast pocket. *When I get lost in Europe, no one will find me.*

He turned and saw his buddy Vinny, who worked part time at Sharkey's, taking a seat beside him.

Rocky took a puff of his cigarette and laid it down in the ashtray. After looking carefully around the room, he pulled an envelope from his jacket pocket and handed it to Vinny. Rocky grabbed his buddy's shoulder. "Like I explained on the phone...I'm goin' away for a while and I want you to take care of that little surprise for Helen. There's plenty of cash here to take care of everything. Just make sure you tell her the surprise is from me!" he said intently.

Vinny nodded his head. "Don't worry about a thing, Rock. I'll take care of it for ya."

Rocky leaned back with a satisfied look on his face. "Bartender, what do I owe ya?"

Later that night, Helen thought about all the attention Sam, the boss, was giving her. She was happy that Rocky was taking a trip and would be out of town for a while. She glanced at the diamond bracelet she got from Sam and her lips turned up in a smile.

What Rock doesn't know won't hurt him, she thought.

The doorbell suddenly rang, jarring her back to the present. She opened the door to find Vinny leaning on the doorframe, a lit cigarette in his mouth.

"What do *you* want?" Helen asked impatiently.

"Rocky says he has something important to give to ya and he wants ya to meet him at Sharkey's."

"What? If it's that important, why didn't he come here himself?" Helen demanded.

"Hey, I don't know nothin'. He just said to tell ya and bring ya down ta see 'em," Vinny said. The cigarette stuck to his bottom lip bounced up and down with each word.

"Oh, all right." Helen begrudgingly walked to the closet and grabbed her coat. "For Chrissakes, he knows how to be a royal pain in the ass!"

Helen shot a look of disgust at Vinny as she reached for the keys on the kitchen shelf. Vinny followed her out the door and she slammed it with a resounding thud. The two rode silently to Sharkey's while Helen wondered what was so damned important that she had to meet Rocky at such an ungodly hour. Vinny parked the car and Helen got out in a huff.

"What the hell's goin' on? It looks like the place is closed," she yelled. "I thought Rocky was going to meet us here."

Vinny unlocked the door and walked in, with Helen following close behind.

"He told me we should wait in case we get here first," he explained.

The place was dimly lit, but Helen could still see that damn shark swimming around the tank. She hated looking at it. It always looked like it was scouting for its next meal. She took off her coat and flung it on a nearby chair. Lighting up a cigarette, she sauntered over to the bar and poured herself a drink. Even in the dim light her new bracelet sparkled brilliantly.

"So, do you know what Rocky wants to give me?" she asked curiously, her back to Vinny.

"He said ya have a big surprise comin' and he wants ya ta know it's from him."

"Really?" Helen turned to find Vinny staring intently at her, a revolver clutched in his hand.

Helen quickly reacted. Her left hand dug into Vinny's eye socket as her right hand forced the gun in a downward position. It fired, and Helen felt a hot piercing pain enter her thigh.

Vinny yelled in agony, cursing as he clutched his eye. "You bitch!"

Helen fell to the floor and crawled behind the bar.

"You fuckin' bitch," he screamed again, "I'm gonna kill you!"

Helen held her breath. Her thigh was now burning, and she could feel the flow of warm blood making its way down her leg.

The bastard must have hit an artery, she thought as she grabbed her thigh and tried to apply pressure. She could see the door to the club's kitchen at the other side of the bar as she slowly dragged herself along the rough wooden floor. Vinny was still cursing and stumbling around, knocking over chairs as he tried to steady himself. Helen slowly made her way on her knees along the back of the bar to the kitchen door. She pushed the swinging doors open and crawled in. Vinny turned quickly, his attention on the kitchen door that was now slightly ajar. He lurched across the length of the bar, clutching to each bar stool as he made his way to the kitchen. Helen crouched beside a cabinet, her heart pounding with fear. Vinny lunged through the door, bursting into the room, his hand over his eye, blood streaming down his face. To his left, on the side of the cabinet, he saw a tiny sparkle in the dim light.

Helen groaned, "Oh, shit..."

Vinny raised the gun and fired. The bullet struck her head and Helen's moan filled the room as she slumped forward.

"I'm not done with you yet," Vinny whispered in contempt.

Chapter 19

Charlie looked at the cartoon drawn by Winston McCoy in the *New York American* and cringed. It depicted many people stuck to what looked like flypaper that was imprinted with the words, "Something For Nothing Ponzi." It was entitled "Fly Time."

He removed his glasses and placed them on the desk.

"Maria, ask Mrs. Ponzi to come to the study, will you?"

"Yes, Mr. Ponzi. Would you like me to bring some coffee?"

"Please...that would be very nice."

Ponzi was dreading this moment, but knew it had finally arrived. He heard the swish of Rose's gown as it swept across the marble floor. Even at such an anxious time he couldn't help but notice her enchanting beauty.

"Charlie, you wanted to see me?"

"Yes, Rose, come sit down, I want to talk to you." The seriousness of the subject was apparent in his voice.

Rose sat down, a frightened look on her face. "What is it, Charlie? Is something wrong?" she asked timidly.

"I'm afraid so. The bank commissioner has closed Hanover Bank. All of my funds are frozen, making it impossible for me to pay my investors. It's become necessary for me to close the business temporarily..."

Rose blanched. "Oh, my God..."

"Now, now, don't get upset. I'll straighten everything out and everything will be fine!" *She was so fragile...like the flowers that climb up the trellis and drop their petals over the porch floor,* he thought.

"But what will you do in the meantime? How will you pay off the investors? I'm frightened.... What will we tell Mama?" her voice trembled.

"Rose, please...calm down. We will tell Mama nothing. For now, we will go about our business as if nothing has changed. Hopefully, the situation will be corrected. Please don't be frightened. Everything will be fine...I promise."

Rose began to cry. Charlie stood and took her in his arms. He felt her body lean into his. "Please don't cry," he said as he held her close. "We may have to take inventory and sell a few things, but it's only temporary."

"I don't care about 'things'.... Will they put you in jail? I couldn't bear it! Please tell me it won't happen. I'm so frightened for you...for *us*." Tears rolled down her cheeks as she looked at him pleadingly.

"Before anything happens, illegalities must be proven. Remember, the people are with us. Just stay calm. It's very important that we stay calm."

Rose wiped her eyes and took a deep breath. "Charlie, can we raise the money ourselves? Sell my jewelry, sell my furs, anything you want...I just want everything to be all right!"

"I am afraid it's not that simple, Rose. Notes are due in excess of six million dollars. All we can do is raise as much cash as possible and continue paying off investors. This might lessen the run and appease the public. All we need is a little more time...just a little more time."

"Well, then, let's do it, Charlie. Right now."

Ponzi picked up the telephone and put the plan in motion while Rose ran upstairs and began cleaning out her jewelry cases. Mama came in and looked around the room. Jewelry boxes lay everywhere, their contents spilling out what looked like a king's ransom. The bed was strewn with furs.

"What's going on, Rose? What are you doing?"

"Oh, Mama, it's all right. I've decided to donate some of my things to the church, to help them raise money for the needy. I've gotten tired of them and plan to buy some new things for myself. If you have anything you would like to add to these, just bring them here. They will be taken away this afternoon."

"How thoughtful of you, dear. Yes, I think I would like to donate a few things myself. Does Charlie know you are doing this?"

"Yes, Mama, Charlie knows. In fact, it was partly his idea."

"He's such a wonderful man. I'm so proud of him!"

Rose turned away just in time. A tear slid down her cheek and she quickly brushed it away. "Yes, I am too," she said softly.

In the study, the phone rang and Charlie quickly picked it up. His white-knuckled hand gripped the receiver. "Oh, come, come, Rico. I've never failed you in the past, have I?" Ponzi spoke quickly. "You'll have your money back in four days."

"Are you kidding, Charlie? I can't let you borrow any more! You have already borrowed seventy-five—"

"All right! I understand!" Ponzi cut him off.

"Don't forget, I want my money back as soon as possible—"

"Listen to me," Ponzi cut him off again, his voice becoming hoarse. "I'll get you your money as soon as I can. I can promise no more!" There was silence on the other end. Charlie spoke apologetically. "You are first on my list, Rico."

"I hope you are as rich as you say you are, Charles Ponzi."

Ponzi hung up and buried his head in his hands. After sitting for a few minutes he stood and walked to the door. He saw a copy of the *Post* on the end table. The headlines read, "PONZI SCHEME IN HOT WATER." Angrily, he ripped the front page to shreds and stormed out of the room.

In the hall he almost collided with Rose carrying an armful of furs, some trailing along the floor. "We'll start with these, Charlie. By the way, I told your mother that we are donating everything to the church. She wants to donate some things too."

"Thank you for not telling her, Rose. It would break her heart!"

"What would break my heart, Charlie?" a voice asked from the top of the stairs. Ponzi, surprised, turned around to face her. "Oh, Mama, I didn't see you there..."

"*Che torto?*"

"Nothing is wrong, Mama."

The elderly woman slowly descended the staircase, a worried look on her face.

"Charlie, *mi amore.* Tell me...what is the trouble?"

"I just have to raise a little cash, Mama...nothing to worry about. I told Rose not to tell you because I know how you would worry."

"Of course I worry about you—I love you! I'm happy you told me." She gave her son a hug and cupped his face in her hands. "Charlie, you are the most wonderful son in the world. I love you. Rose loves you. We will find a way to solve your *torto*, all of us together."

Rose joined the two and put her arms around them. "She's right, Charlie. We can do it together."

Charlie knew it would not be that easy. Raising enough money to cover a few day's payoffs would be no small task. The facts remained: his credit had dried up and he had lost all his credibility. Ponzi walked into the living room with both women following behind and gazed around at the magnificent pieces of art he had managed to accumulate.

"All this should raise a good amount of money," said Rose. "I'll call the art dealer and tell him we are tired of it and ask him to sell it for us. It's perfect...his office is out of state, so we can do it confidentially," she insisted.

"Yes, you're right," Charlie agreed, "but we must be careful how we dispose of our valuables. If word got out, it would certainly cause more negative speculation."

"That's right. The beautiful part is that we have many paintings and antiques. It was smart of you to invest so wisely, Charlie."

"I just wanted you and Mama to be surrounded by beautiful things. As soon as business straightens out, I'll get them back...I promise."

Rose called the art dealer and made arrangements for the sale. Mama hugged Charlie, knowing full well how devastating this was for him. She held him tightly and patted his back.

"Mama, I'm glad you are here. Rose is going to need you," he whispered in her ear. He knew he could count on Mama. She was from the old country, just as he was, and they were as strong as the olive trees that grew in their yard in Parma. They stood their ground, and year after year survived the wind, the cold, and even the heat. "We can do it, too," Charlie assured himself.

Chapter 20

Rocky finished packing his suitcase and slammed down the lid. Grabbing his topcoat, he walked to the door and shut off the light. Turning, he looked around the room. The neon sign across the street reflected its light through the window onto the wall.

"It'll be real nice to get away for a while. I'm getting tired of this dump anyway." He shut the door and walked down the dark stairway and out onto the street. To his surprise, Marco was standing outside the building lighting a cigarette.

"Hey, Rock, I was just about to go up and ask ya if ya want to go out for a drink!"

"Well, maybe a quick one," Rocky answered.

"Great, I got the car around the corner."

Marco threw his cigarette down and the two men walked around the corner and got into the car. As the car sped down the street, Marco shot a look at Rocky.

"Did ya take care of that job the boss gave ya?"

"Yeah, yeah, it's all taken care of...he's history. Why do you ask?" Rocky asked curiously.

"No reason," Marco said, directing his attention to the road. "I know it was a big hit...I was just wonderin'."

The two rode in silence for several blocks until they came to a stop for a red light. Rocky noticed two wise-guys standing on the corner. Marco motioned to them.

"Hey, there's Fingers and Aldo."

Marco cranked down the window and yelled, "Hey, you guys want to go for a drink wit' us?"

The two guys ran over to the car and jumped into the back seat. Fingers leaned over the front seat. "Where we goin'?"

Aldo offered, "How about the bar on the North Road?"

Marco nodded in agreement. "Sounds good to me...how about you, Rock?"

"All right with me, but let's not take all night."

"All right...all right," Marco yelled, "relax, will ya?"

The four rode down the highway. Rocky leaned over and switched on the radio. He didn't feel comfortable with the two capos sitting behind him, but he shook off the feeling. The car turned off a ramp and stopped alongside the road.

Rocky asked, "Why are we stoppin' here?"

Marco shot him an annoyed look. "I have to take a leak, OK?"

Marco got out of the car and started walking into a cornfield. With his back to the road, he stopped and began to pull his pants zipper down. At the same time, a gunshot broke the silence of the cold night.

Marco murmured under his breath, "Sorry, Rock...business is business."

He pulled up his zipper and walked back to the vehicle and looked inside.

"Jesus Christ! What a mess! Couldn't you guys whack him a little neater?"

Fingers yelled, "Who the hell are you, the fuckin' cleaning lady? Forget the car—just get in and let's get the hell outta here!"

Rocky was slumped over on the front seat, and the windshield and dashboard were splattered with blood.

Marco muttered, "Sonovabitch... I feel like shit! Rock was a good guy. Hittin' one of our own, it feels against the rules...ya know?"

Aldo laughed. "Tell it to the priest! If the boss says, 'do it,' we do it. Get this hearse movin'...we got to get to the Ice House fast!"

Marco carefully climbed into the driver's seat and put the car in high gear. When they reached the Ice House, Fingers and Aldo carried Rocky's body in through the back door with Marco following behind. Fingers yelled to one of the capos inside.

"Put him on ice. They're pourin' cement for the new bank next week, and the boss wants him in there!"

"Funny, ain't it...Rocky always wanted to be where the money was," Marco remarked thoughtfully.

"Yeah, it's Goddamned prophetic, ain't it?" Aldo added sarcastically.

"Hey! How about that drink?" Aldo asked, unaffected by the event.

"Take the spare car in the back and follow me out to the dump. We'll take care of the car first," Marco reminded the others.

"You got it," Aldo answered.

The two sedans made their way to the dump where they parked a good distance from each other and the three men got out. Marco removed the plates as Aldo poured gasoline in and around the vehicle. Fingers threw a match and the three stood at a distance, watching the car burn, then finally explode. The three jumped into the waiting sedan and took off.

"We'll have to drink a toast to that poor bastard," Fingers admitted.

Marco agreed. "Yeah, it's tough getting rid of a *compagno*!"

"Hey, you win a few, you lose a few...right? Besides, Rock was a two-faced rat!" Aldo added.

Marco shook his head. "I guess...me, I was OK wit' him!"

Later, in his office, Sam sat at his desk mulling over the fact that he hadn't heard from Helen in a few days.

I wonder what kind of crap she's pulling, he thought as he angrily chewed on his cigar. There was a slight tap on the door.

"Alright to come in?" a voice asked nervously.

"Yah, Marco, come on in and shut the door behind you."

Marco obediently entered and waited for a signal to sit down. The boss waved his hand.

"Sit down," he ordered in a gruff voice. "So... how did the job go? Everything copacetic?" he asked with a smile.

"Yah, boss, everything's cool. Rocky's history. Everything was taken care of...no problems."

"Anytime now we should be hearin' about Allen's body bein' discovered, thanks to Rocky. One less Fed is a good thing," he muttered. "Where's Rock now?" he snapped.

"He's at the Ice House."

"Good job, Marco...good job. I got a lot of respect for you. I know you and him were kinda close."

Marco lowered his head. "My first loyalty is to the family, one hundred percent. *Sangue del meo Sangue*...blood of our blood...the oath we all took to work for the good of the family...always!"

"That's right!" Sam sat down and leaned back in his chair. "Have you seen his girl Helen lately?" he asked nonchalantly.

"No, I haven't, Boss. I know she likes to hang out at Sharkey's a lot," Marco answered, scratching his head.

"So I've heard. It's a hotspot, and I got a feelin' she thrives on that."

"Yah, Boss...you got that right! She's a hot ticket, sometimes a little more than even ol' Rock could handle!"

Sam cleared his throat. "I gather that... well, see you at the meeting tomorrow night. We got a few important things to discuss. Eight o'clock sharp at Sharkey's." Sam stood, giving a signal of dismissal.

"Sure, Boss." Marco rose and quickly left the room.

The next evening, Sam walked into Sharkey's and surveyed the place. Several members of the gang were huddled around one of the back tables. He sauntered over to the bar and leaned against one of the stools.

"So, Vinny...what do you know?"

"Nothin' new, Boss," Vinny answered as he grabbed a glass and began to fix the head capo's favorite drink.

"What the hell happened to your eye? It looks like you did two rounds with Dempsey!"

"I had a little misunderstandin' with a friend," Vinny answered. "I got the better end of the deal."

At that moment, Marco walked over and leaned in. "Just want ya to know not everybody knows that Rocky bought the farm."

Hearing this, Vinny nervously dropped the lemon slice, quickly scooped it up, and hastily dropped it into the glass. Sam picked up his drink, and the two joined the ominous group. Vinny turned and wiped the sweat from his forehead. "Poor Rock, he didn't see that comin'!" he whispered to himself.

At the table, the group ordered a round of drinks from Vinny as the boss lit up a cigarette and tossed the match in the overflowing ashtray. He listened intently as each gave his report. As he gazed around the room, a shimmering object in the water tank caught his eye. He picked up his drink and walked over to the tank for a closer look. Lying on the bottom of the tank was a half devoured forearm with the bracelet he had given Helen, sparkling brilliantly, as the shark innocently swam around, a menacing look in his eyes.

Chapter 21

Along with several auditors, Joe methodically worked his way through the records of the Hanover, the Old Colony, the Polish Industrial Association, and Cosmopolitan Banks. In all, four banks were closed. Joe found unqualified loans were registered in Ponzi's name, along with accounts to a Lucy Martelli, whose account was overdrawn. Joe filed a $4,764,000 suit against the thirteen directors. After more digging, he found that President Mitchell owed the bank $130,000, which he had obtained with unsecured loans. The situation had become a huge mess...there was no doubt Fidelity Bank would be next. The problem had eaten its way through like a cancer, pervading the entire Boston banking system. Few directors or officers would emerge clean. Joe found many had helped Ponzi in obtaining illegal loans and others had helped themselves. The rotten stench of greed could no longer be concealed—all must be dragged out into the open and exposed. The only question in Joe's mind was: who would be next?

Joe dug into his scrambled eggs and picked up the morning paper. The headlines screamed, "BANK OFFICIAL COMMITS SUICIDE." He put down the newspaper and closed his eyes. Guilt covered him like a heavy wet blanket. Were his actions instrumental in this latest turn of events? The radio announcer interrupted his thoughts.

"Governor Coolidge has just made the following statement: 'I have complete faith in Commissioner Allen's decision to close several of Boston's banks. He informed me a general house cleaning was in order. Ponzi has been found to have borrowed large sums of money from some of these banks on straw names. Although the bank closings have brought about a storm of criticisms upon his shoulders, the Commissioner has my loyal support, together with the support of many prominent citizens. Our banking system has found itself in the most serious financial condition in its history. In this crisis the Commissioner has proved equal to the emergency. He has shown he is neither afraid of threats, nor subject to influence pressed on him by offenders of sound banking business. Commissioner Allen is an efficient, thorough, and capable man, and the most satisfactory appointment I have made during this administration. Thank you.'"

Joe leaned over and turned off the radio. If he didn't hurry, he would be late for work.

On School Street, he observed a mob pressing itself toward the Security Exchange office front. The police officers tried to maintain calm as the seething crowd bickered and cursed amongst themselves.

"Will you all please go home?" an officer shouted. "There will be no business transactions here today."

"What about our money?" someone shouted. "To hell with the interest...we just want our initial investment back!"

"Yeah, give us our money back!" The chant rose to a roar. "We want Ponzi, we want Ponzi..."

"Ponzi is not here. Go back to your homes. You will all be notified if there are any refunds."

Slowly the crowd dispersed.

"I'm glad the bastard only got me for a few bucks," Joe overheard one officer confide to the other.

"Well, if you think these people are pissed, you ought to see the lynch mob at Old Colony. Now *there's* a genuine reason to be mad as hell!"

"Jesus, here it is August and already the roof's falling in on that big shot Ponzi ," said the first. "It's hard to believe all this happening in just eight short months!"

"Well...I just wonder where it's all going to end," the Irishman shot back, slapping his club against his hand.

Joe didn't want to speculate, but he knew one thing: even with the negative reports, some still believed in the so-called 'financial wizard.' He decided to drive to his hometown of Springfield to see if the effects of the scandal had drifted to the west of the commonwealth and came upon Andrew Lapardo, a friend of Charlie's.

"Your closing of banks is an outrage. Ponzi should have been allowed to negotiate the $1,500,000 time deposit that he had with the Hanover Bank and couldn't be drawn upon until the 27th of the month," he shouted. "There are several local investors who would still be winners if they hadn't lost on the notes they were holding!"

"Ponzi is a fraud," shot back Allen. "You know it and I know it!"

"That's not true! Ponzi is a genius, ahead of his time. He wanted to help the average person. Why, he even planned to open an office here near Court Square before all this investigating began!"

"For God's sake, get your head out of the sand, Lapardo! Ponzi is only out for himself," Joe answered, walking away. He headed for the police station to have a few words with Chief Quilty.

"Are there any signs of the Ponzi pyramid in Springfield, Chief?"

"Right now I'm investigating a copycat company called Domestic and Foreign Securities and Trading Company with offices in the Hitchcock Building on Main Street. A man claiming to be a representative of that company visited my home with an investment offer à la the Ponzi scam with fifty per cent interest in forty-five days and one hundred per cent interest in ninety days."

"Did you check it out?" asked Joe.

"Yes, I did—and I was met by the manager, Gaetano G. Cataldo. He insisted I was visited by an impostor, and that anyone promising such interest was lying. In fact, he said they do not send out any agents. He insisted he didn't want to be dragged into the Ponzi mess. Cataldo maintained the company's purpose was to deal with bonds in a legitimate way. He even stated the company was given a charter in Boston and he was named treasurer of the corporation."

"How about if we check if this Cataldo guy has a record?" Allen suggested.

"Of course."

The chief began pulling out files. After some searching, they found a 1910 report on a Gaetano G. Cataldo of Acushnet Avenue being arrested for larceny.

"What was he charged with?" Allen asked inquisitively.

"He took $200 from a young elevator boy who had received $600 insurance money for an on the job injury."

"Interesting," Allen said thoughtfully. "So he does have a record."

"Yes, he was found guilty and fined $225 by Judge Heady," answered the chief.

"Perhaps you should issue a warning to Springfield residents against investment promoters. People should carefully check the credentials of those offering investment services," Allen suggested.

The chief agreed, nodding his head. "That sounds practical, Commissioner. I'll do that."

Chapter 22

"Come in," yelled Richard Grozier in response to the knock on his office door. The door opened, filling the room with the sounds of the newsroom. Edward Dunn sank into a chair and wiped his brow.

"It's damned hot this morning," he said with disgust.

Dunn held the post of City Editor and was well-liked and respected by his peers.

"Well, what did you come up with?" asked Grozier. "More than a weather report, I hope."

"I've checked with our *Post* correspondent in Paris. He says there have been no extensive sales of international reply coupons either there or in Switzerland. Washington reports that less than $10,000 worth of coupons were redeemed so far this year. So I'd say this Ponzi is full of shit...and so is his company!"

"It would seem so," pondered Grozier. "All right, then...let's get this story in print. The sooner the better!"

"You know, Richard, I think once this all gets out, it will be a nail in Ponzi's coffin."

"Don't be too sure of that. The guy's got a lot to lose if he throws in the towel."

Grozier shook his head in disgust. "We've got to expose him for what he is—a greedy bastard with no conscience."

In his office, Dunn rolled a sheet of paper into his typewriter and began typing.

The title shouted out the cold, hard facts. "This will light a fire under his ass," Dunn mumbled to himself.

After calling to check on facts and typing feverishly for a good part of the morning, Dunn completed his printed attack and leaned back with a sigh. Just making the twelve o'clock deadline, he pulled the paper out and hurried to deliver his bomb to the print setter.

"Let's see how well Mr. Ponzi digests his dinner tonight!"

Dunn walked into the type setting room and dropped the article on the table.

"Take good care of this, Ben. I want it to have star billing: front page headlines and story; the works!"

"Yes, sir, Mr. Dunn. A hot piece of news, is it?"

"Hotter than a firecracker! Let's just say that I think it's the beginning of the end."

"I'll give it top priority!" Ben said as he began setting the type.

Dunn returned to his desk and re-read the Paris report on reply coupons.

"If he's not making his money this way, then *how* is he making it?" he wondered aloud. The phone rang and Dunn picked it up. It was a newspaper in Montreal answering one of the telegrams he sent out coast-to-coast. They reported that a similar scheme was tried there. Dunn was thrilled with the new lead, and immediately called two of his star reporters into his office. Harold Wheeler and Herbert Baldwin quickly strode in and sat down.

"I want you both to go to Montreal. I think we might have a lead on our friend Ponzi."

"I can be ready in a couple of hours, Mr. Dunn," Wheeler declared.

"Same with me," added Baldwin.

"Get the facts and get them pronto! This could be our big break. I'll give you all the necessary information before you leave."

The two nodded and left the office immediately.

In his office, Ponzi read the headlines in the *Boston Post* and decided once and for all to pay a personal visit to Eddie Dunn. Charlie sauntered into the newspaper building, accompanied by a group of sympathizers. Since the facts were finally exposed, Ponzi conceded that the *Post* had indeed unearthed the truth.

"Mr. Dunn, you are absolutely right, the International Reply Coupon was merely a cover to protect my secret plan of operations. Why are you persecuting me? Why are you hounding me? Why are you always printing these lies about me?" Ponzi demanded.

"It's very simple. I don't think you're honest," Dunn calmly replied.

"I am not a crook," Ponzi responded indignantly. "I have kept all my promises, and my investors have all made money! You just don't want to see all these people get ahead, thanks to me!"

"We are just trying to get at the truth. If you are as honest as you claim, you won't mind us investigating your affairs. This is all being done in the public interest, and if you're as honest as you say, Ponzi, then you have nothing to fear," retorted Dunn.

Ponzi stood and pounded the desk with his fist. "I've been honest all my life!"

"You're not that honest! You've done time, Ponzi, and you know it!"

Dunn stunned the group around them, bluffing the already flustered visitor. Ponzi stood speechless for a moment, shocked at the editor's charges. Trying to compose himself, he answered indignantly, "I have been honest all my life! I have *never* 'done time.' I'm an honest man!"

With that declaration, Ponzi and his supporters filed out of the office and the normal din in the room resumed.

Later that afternoon, Dunn visited the office of the Attorney General.

"Does this picture remind you of anyone?" asked the Attorney General.

After careful scrutiny, Dunn nodded his head and replied, "Except for the moustache, he looks just like Charles Ponzi."

"That's what we think. It's from the Rogues Gallery in Montreal." He was sure he was hot on the trail of something big.

When Wheeler and Baldwin arrived in Montreal, they had several problems. Although the picture looked like Ponzi in the Rogues Gallery, those working at the Penitentiary or the Police Department had never heard of the man.

Figuring that Ponzi would probably have started his get rich quick scheme by involving his Italian friends, the two visited the Italian section of Montreal to investigate. They visited shop after shop with a photo, asking anyone present if they had ever seen the man pictured. All answered negatively until they happened on a particular shop where a heavy-set mustached man was sweeping the floor behind the counter. Baldwin held out the photo to the man, who cleared his throat, took a fast look at the picture, and answered, his eyes shifting nervously, "No...I never saw a' him."

"Thanks for your time," Baldwin said, and they left the shop.

Outside, Wheeler looked at Baldwin and asked, "What do you think?"

"I've got a gut feeling he's lying through his teeth," Baldwin answered.

"No shit," said Wheeler.

Baldwin nodded, and turned to note the family name on the shop window.

"Let's track down family members and see if any are willing to tell the truth," he cunningly suggested.

After checking the name in the telephone book, they were soon knocking on the door of a small cottage in a quiet section of the city. They knocked several times until a short woman with gray hair and a ruddy complexion opened the door a crack to ask what they wanted.

"Ma'am, we just talked with your husband at the store, and he said you could give us some information on this man that you know." Baldwin withdrew Ponzi's picture from his pocket and the woman looked at it briefly.

"Oh, yes, we'a know him. His a'name is Charles Bianchi... he looks a li'l different there because'a he shaved off'a his mustache," she added.

"What do you know about him?" pressed Wheeler.

"Well... he was'a once arrested for forgin' a check, but'a he serv'a his time, and then he was'a freed."

Baldwin tipped his hat. "Thank you for your time, Ma'am. You've been a big help."

They grabbed a cab and hurried back to the police station.

"Did you ever hear of a 'Charles Bianchi?'" they asked the captain in charge.

"Yes, we know of Bianchi. He used to work in a bank here until he was convicted of theft. I'm sure we have record of it."

They scoured the records. Finally, Wheeler's hands shook as he pulled out a file.

"I think this is it," he said over his shoulder.

"In 1908, Ponzi, then known as 'Charles Bianchi' and working in a bank, got together with the bank manager and organized a financial scheme. They promised to pay depositors the highest interest rates, and even offered to send money to family members in Italy: money that never got there. When the police and bank examiners started to close in, his partner took off to Mexico and left Ponzi holding the bag. He did three years in St.Vincent De Paul jail and was released in July of 1910."

"How the hell do you like that?" Baldwin murmured under his breath.

"I think we got a scoop! Let's get back and do something about it!" Wheeler shouted, his eyes sparkling with satisfaction.

The two decided to confront Ponzi at his home in Lexington. With story in hand, together with a photograph of a mustached Bianchi from Montreal's Rogues Gallery and a photograph of Boston's Ponzi with an applied mustached, they rang his doorbell.

"We'd like to speak to Mr. Ponzi," Wheeler requested of the butler. They were shown into the foyer. Ponzi soon entered with a cigar in his hand.

"What can I do for you?"

Wheeler handed him the story and the pictures. They waited pensively for a reaction.

"Ha, ha, ha! This is ridiculous," Ponzi replied. He raised his voice angrily. "Where did you get this pack of lies?" he demanded. "I assure you, I have *never* been in Montreal, and I have *never* been arrested. If the *Post* insists on publishing this garbage I will slap them with so many lawsuits that they will go bankrupt!"

"These are documented facts, sir. We just thought we would make you aware of our findings before we make them public," stated Baldwin.

"Get out of my house! I've been patient with you long enough! Get out!" Ponzi screamed in frustration.

That day, the greatest news story of the year was printed, winning the *Boston Post* the Pulitzer Prize. All Ponzi's offices were immediately closed to depositors.

Although he wasn't sure of the ramifications, Ponzi decided to meet with the press and make a full confession. "Yes, it's true: I, Charles Ponzi, also known as Charles Bianchi, was sentenced to three years in prison for forgery in Montreal. During 1911 and 1912, I also served two years in Atlanta, Georgia, for violating the United States Immigration law. I was guilty of bringing five Italians into this country over the Canadian border. I was committed within ten days of my release from the Montreal prison, where I was freed after twenty months for good behavior." Ponzi, who had tried to stay debonair and jovial throughout all the difficulties, began to weep.

"Society owes me a chance to redeem my past," he continued. "My greatest sorrow, however, is having my wife Rose learn about my past record. I have never told her about these things," he added sadly. "I only hope she will understand."

At the close of the interview, Charlie bid the reporters farewell and showed them out. He closed the door and found Rose standing at the bottom of the staircase.

"I'm so sorry, Rose. I never meant to hurt you. I had hoped you would never find out about my past..."

"I still love you, Charlie. I will be there for you no matter what happens," Rose answered as she walked toward her husband with her arms outstretched. The two held each other tightly and Charlie covered his young wife's face with kisses.

Chapter 23

Joe tried to comprehend why so many well-educated and astute bankers became corrupt. *Was it the times, which were filled with optimism and enthusiasm, or was it a simple matter of greed and the lax laws that governed the country's banking system? It's 1920—people are filled with confidence, with the need to live-it-up, with the desire to grab for the brass ring,* he theorized. But at the Attorney General's office he saw a different kind of world. Angry crowds of note-holders stormed the office yelling revenge on Ponzi and on Charles Brightwell, head of the Old Colony, who admitted his bank was insolvent.

"Let us have Brightwell and Ponzi," the furious crowd demanded. The sergeant-at-arms immediately called in the state police to help quell the mob.

At his home in Lexington, Charlie saw the writing on the wall. He knew it was over and it was time to...what was that American expression?...'Face the music.'

One of Ponzi's greatest fears was deportation. The subject was brought up by a newspaper reporter, and Ponzi read the Immigration Commissioner's reply:

"If Ponzi committed a crime within five years of his entrance into the United States, he would be liable for deportation. I understand he went to Canada immediately upon his arrival here; therefore, the five years limit would be counted from the time he entered this country from Canada. If he has a criminal record in Canada, he probably came into this country without inspection. If he did that, then he made false and untruthful statements and is here unlawfully. At the end of the present investigation, a report will be sought on his status as a possible undesirable alien."

"Rose, come here. I must speak with you," Charlie said gently.

Rose sat down next to her embattled husband. His voice cracked as he spoke. "I want you to arrange passage for Mama back to Italy, and then I want you to move back to your parents' house."

"No, don't ask me to do that! I can't leave you!" she pleaded.

"You must," he insisted. "I must surrender myself to the authorities."

"No, I won't let you go... I love you..." she sobbed uncontrollably.

"I love you too, more than life itself," he said. "But...but for now you must take care of yourself and Mama. I'll make bail and very soon we will be together, I promise!"

That afternoon Ponzi called his attorney and together they walked to District Attorney Gallagher's office.

"I'm unable to meet my liabilities," Ponzi stated with a hushed voice, "and therefore I am willing to surrender." The three went to the Federal Building where they met with United States Marshall Duane.

Duane threw the book at Ponzi. "You are hereby charged with using the mails to commit fraud, and you will be held in custody awaiting bonds of $25,000."

"Bail will be forthcoming today," assured Ponzi.

"We have also just been notified the State Attorney General Weston Allen is on his way to municipal court to obtain a warrant for your arrest. Therefore, if bail is furnished, you will immediately be arrested on a warrant charging you with larceny on fifty counts. I expect your bail will then be increased to $50,000 dollars," Duane added.

Ponzi's confidence was shattered. The bushel-basket millionaire's bubble had burst! He was suddenly reduced to a nervous, weary-eyed man, fearful of the future. The famous Ponzi smile was gone, as well as the jaunty straw hat and cane. He made a frantic effort to find someone to furnish bail, but it was futile. Hour after hour passed by as Charlie paced the floor or sat with his head in his hands, but no one would provide the funds.

A week ago, I was the idol of the city, he thought, completely stunned. *Today... I will be staying in jail!*

"May I call my wife?" he asked.

"Use the telephone in my office," Marshall Duane replied.

Ponzi dialed home and Rose answered.

"Rose, I posted my bail, but I will be out of the city for the night...it's a matter of business," he said.

"All right, Charlie. But please hurry home," she replied. Rose was simply too young and naïve to suspect anything.

Ponzi sat silently as the group made the trip to jail in a taxi. Once there, he made a fast run to the entrance to avoid the photographers. He was close to the point of collapsing as he was brought to the receiving office to be fingerprinted, photographed, and booked. He sat in a chair and tried to answer the questions fired at him as the full extent of what was happening hit him like a ton of bricks. His gaze fell upon the calendar hanging on the wall. A look of terror crept across his face as he realized what day it was, and his superstitious nature filled him with fear.

"It's Friday the 13th," he said with a shudder. "This is a bad omen!"

"Take a shower and change into this uniform," he was instructed by one of the surly guards. After changing into the drab clothing, Charlie quietly did what he was told and was soon shown to his cell.

The evening meal consisted of a breaded veal chop, French fried potatoes, toast, a pot of coffee, a bottle of ginger ale, and a cantaloupe. Ponzi read the evening newspaper and then called for a guard.

"Could you possibly get me a pipe?" he asked.

"I'll see what I can do," the guard replied.

A short while later the guard returned with a pipe, which was purchased near the jail by a sympathetic guard going off duty. Ponzi smoked and quietly meditated. It was later that he finally fell asleep. Unknown to him, several of his close friends called at the jail but were refused a visit. They were told Ponzi would not be allowed to see anyone for the present. He lay asleep in his small, starkly furnished cell, a far cry from the royal bedroom he had shared with his wife Rose.

Chapter 24

On August 14th the headlines read, "ANOTHER BOSTON BANK CLOSED IN CONNECTION WITH THE PONZI CASE." The Polish Industrial Association, the affairs of which were woven in with the Hanover Trust, was shut down per order of Bank Commissioner Joseph Allen. After investigating, Allen found that Henry Chmielinski, president of the Hanover Trust, was also president of the Polish Industrial Association, and James E. O'Connell, secretary of the Polish Bank, was an official in the Hanover Trust.

"I have found that many loans are of doubtful value—some were bad, and there is little cash left. The last statement of this bank showed deposits of $352,000," Allen said. "Also, creditors of the Old Colony have filed an involuntary petition in bankruptcy against the concern today."

Joe watched in utter dismay as more crowds of angry note-holders again stormed Attorney General Weston Allen's office. The Attorney filled Joe in on what was happening.

"Today, Assistant Attorney General Hurwitz and Attorney McIsaac, council for Charles Ponzi, appeared before Judge Bennett in Municipal Court in an attempt to reach an agreement for bail under the fifty-three count blanket warrant the state secured provided he should be released, but Attorney McIsaac was insistent on $25,000, so no agreement has been reached. Also today, representatives for Slater and Witte, attorneys in the first involuntary bankruptcy petition filed against Ponzi, made arrangements whereby next Tuesday Judge Morton of the Federal Court will give a hearing relative to the appointment of a receiver. In the meantime, three intervening petitions in bankruptcy were filed in connection with the case."

After the conference, Joe and Weston Allen took a sip of their coffee and tried to relax. The whole Ponzi thing had erupted into a three-ring circus. His assistant, Hurwitz, walked in and sat down.

"Christ, what a nightmare!" Hurwitz moaned. "It looks like we're going to have a tangle of suits on our hands. The fed, the state, individual bankruptcies...you name it!" He ran his fingers through his hair in frustration.

"Who would have imagined one man could have caused all this shit?" the AG asked. "The joke is that the man is an idiot! He was totally ignorant of business procedures. Would you believe he didn't even own a typewriter or an adding machine?" he added.

"You've got to be kidding!" replied Hurwitz, incredulously.

Joe looked at Weston with disbelief.

"It's true! With the huge amount of money flowing into that dingy office, he would have kept a huge staff of accountants busy. But instead he hired a handful of girls and a few young fellows to basically shovel the money into bushel-baskets and write out the notes."

"Well, how the hell did the guy keep track of what he made?" questioned Hurwitz.

"That's just it...he didn't keep one goddamned record!" Joe countered. "He just guessed at figures."

Both men turned their attention to the door as a guard entered.

"Sir, there is a large group of investors here that want to speak to you," he announced.

"Send the first person in," Weston instructed.

A World War veteran bearing scars from his many war wounds and suffering from tuberculosis limped in. "I have a note for $750 I invested with Ponzi. I had saved that money to go to Arizona to help my weak lungs. But I survived the battle overseas, and I can survive this. I just feel sorry for the couple behind me," he said.

An Italian couple walked in. The woman's eyes were swollen from weeping. "We gave Ponzi $2,600. We were planning to use it to go back to Italy. We met with Ponzi and he assured us we would have a great deal more money when he paid us. Now...we have nothing!" The woman began to sob. Joe shook his head in disgust and left.

By week's end, Joe was told hundreds of men and women had visited the office. Some were young factory workers, some poorly dressed people, and some fashionably gowned women. All told pathetic stories of years of savings lost. Most investors were angry and even wept. Some were so ashamed they were duped that they resented being questioned. One of Ponzi's principal assistants stated that two-thirds of the members of the Boston Police Department were investors.

In the Lexington mansion, Rose read the headlines in disbelief. "PONZI SURRENDERS!"

"This can't be...I don't believe it!" Rose dropped the paper as her eyes widened with fear.

Mama came in and sat down at the table. "What is it, Rose? You look as though you've seen a ghost!"

"Mama, Charlie has been arrested! He surrendered to the authorities yesterday!"

"What?! That's...that'sa impossible..." the old woman sputtered.

"It's true, Mama. It says that no one came forth with his bail, so he is being held at the Cambridge jail."

"You did not a'know about this?" the woman asked.

"No! He called late yesterday afternoon and said he would be out of town for the night... oh, my God...what will we do?"

"It's all right, Rosa. I'm'a sure Charlie will get in touch'a with us and tell us'a what we should'a do," the old woman said reassuringly.

At that moment the doorbell rang. Rose answered it.

"Mrs. Ponzi, I am Attorney McIsaac. I've been chosen to represent Charlie."

Rose showed him into the dining room. He extended his hand to Rose and turned and acknowledged Ponzi's mother. "Charlie has asked me to tell you that he is very sorry about the turn of events. He was certain he would be released on bail, but this has not happened."

"What do you expect *will* happen?" Rose asked.

"At this point we are not sure...of course, when we go to trial, we will do our best to prove Charlie innocent of mail fraud. However, there have been many bankruptcy petitions and a receiver has just been named."

"What does-a that mean?" the elder Mrs. Ponzi questioned.

"It means that the courts may order this house and its furnishings sold and the monies divided amongst the petitioners."

"Oh, no," moaned Rose.

"Thank you, Mr. McIsaac, for'a coming and explainin' a things to us," the old woman said as she slowly stood and offered her hand.

McIsaac tried to smile, but found it difficult. "I'll keep you abreast of the situation. In the meantime, perhaps you should find new living quarters, just to be on the safe side."

The attorney left and both women sat and looked at each other, unable to speak. Rose finally broke the silence. "I can always go back and live with my parents, but what will *you* do, Mama?"

"Don'ta you worry about me. I have'a enough money to go back'a home to Italy. But right'a now, I will stay here in case'a my son needs me."

Outside, a crowd of angry people gathered on the sidewalk, hoping to get an opportunity to complain to someone—*anyone*—about their misfortunes. Rose pressed her fist against her mouth to stifle a sob. She was so frightened without her Charlie. How did this happen? Why couldn't he have been happy with the way things were, in the beginning when they first met? She wished it was all a horrible nightmare, and she would soon wake up and find everything the way it used to be. Rose lowered her head and cried. Teardrops fell on her satin dress, leaving stains like tracks leading to a far bitter time to come.

Chapter 25

On the advice of his counsel, Ponzi pleaded guilty in Federal court to using the mail to commit fraud in hopes of receiving a lighter sentence. He was given a sentence of five years in Plymouth jail. Rose was notified that the $40,000 mansion would be added to other belongings of Ponzi's and sold, with the collected monies given to the receiver to meet the demand of some of Ponzi's creditors.

The huge crowds of people that at one time flocked to the Lexington home to get a glimpse of the get-rich-quick genius now repeated the pilgrimage to buy at auction Ponzi's personal belongings. The palatial home, filled with magnificent paintings, expensive furniture made of the finest wood, heavy window draperies, musical instruments, lamps, and antique rugs was dismantled like a giant crossword puzzle and its contents sold to the highest bidders. It was stated that probably only half of the original cost of the items would be realized.

During one of their visits to Charlie, Rose told him that she and Mama had found a small apartment where they moved their meager belongings. The two visited Charlie twice a week without fail. Ponzi was told that a voluntary bankruptcy petition was filed on behalf of his friends Simon Swig, vice president of the defunct Tremont Trust Company, and Max Mitchell, president of the Cosmopolitan Trust Company. They, along with several others, were hauled before 'Poor Debtors' court in Boston. Ponzi testified in court that three-quarters of the members of the Boston Police Department had invested in his get-rich-quick scheme. It was common knowledge that many had been caught in the collapse of the bubble, but no one had guessed how very large the number actually was.

Ponzi found prison life interesting. His favorite time of day was the evening. After dinner he would lay on his cot and read the various articles still being written about him, and strangely enough enjoyed the notoriety. One December night, he read aloud with amusement the *New York Times* account of his life in prison.

"Six months ago, Charles Ponzi ate caviar and terrapin from plates of silver. Across the table, his pretty little wife poured tea or coffee from a costly service. His butler, pompous and correct, passed the cup, and life was like the sparkling burgundy that glistened in the goblets.

"Yesterday Ponzi ate roast pork, turnips, onions, and potatoes; a good meal, but humble. A brother convict, shaven and shorn, passed tin cups, and life was as the prison coffee…dark and bitter. At home his wife bowed her head below mistletoe and sobbed."

Ponzi looked up from his paper and thought of Rose and how much he loved her. A quiet tear rolled down his cheek.

"'Ponzi is a prisoner among prisoners—no worse, no better than a great many of his brother convicts,' said Sheriff Blake of the Plymouth Jail. 'In his spare time, he writes poems—clever little things to his wife and his fellow inmates. Sometimes they are philosophical and sometimes humorous. Occasionally he turns cynic and then again he romances. The inmates say it is a mean pen Ponzi scribbles—but I'm inclined to believe it is a prolific one. Just now he is wondering about securing copyrights pending the publication of his first book.'

"Between manual labor and literary pursuits, Ponzi is pretty busy. 'Later I'm going to let him take charge of our library. We have some five or six hundred books, and are badly in need of cataloging them in order.'

"It was during the Christmas entertainment presented in the forenoon that Ponzi scored the biggest hit here. Original jingles, written for the occasion and delivered in his own inimitable style, brought down the house. Rhyming on the foibles of the inmates and jailers in lyrics was the feature of the program."

At his table in the dingy cell, Ponzi leaned back and smiled to himself. "I think I will send a Christmas greeting to all my creditors."

He took a sheet of his newly purchased stationary, a gift from his wife. On the top were engraved the words, "Charles Ponzi—Plymouth, Massachusetts." He took his pen in hand and wrote:

"To my thousands of creditors I send holiday greetings of good cheer. I hope that the miscarriage of your investments does not mar the spirit of the Christmas season—I ask you to look forward with me to the day I will be released from this jail, a free man, and aid you in recovering your losses. In closing, if anyone has a response to this Yuletide message, please send a word of sympathy and encouragement to my wife and mother."

Sincerely, Charles Ponzi

He put his pen down just in time to hear a guard yelling, "Lights out!" He laid down on his side and pulled the blanket up to this neck, and satisfied, fell asleep.

Epilogue

Joe and Hart sat in their living room and silently read the *Post*. Hart stole a look at Joe, and shook her head.

"The *Post* says that after Ponzi's assets are finally distributed, his creditors will receive only twelve cents on the dollar! Is that true?"

"That's right. And yet, there are those that believe if I hadn't intervened, and if the authorities had left him alone, Ponzi would have paid back all the money he had promised."

"You did what you had to do, Joe," Hart insisted. "Ponzi's greed and corruption nearly crept into the entire banking system! Thank God for your wisdom and fast actions! How many other innocent victims would have been wiped out financially? I think that most people realize you are a hero. Because of your actions many of the unsubstantial banking laws have been changed. This will most assuredly protect millions of people in the future!"

Taking her husband's hand in hers, she said, "I'm so proud of you, dear. You've done a wonderful thing for your fellow man, and I'm sure *someday* everyone will realize it!"

"My dear Hart...you're very sweet." He leaned over and kissed her.

Acknowledgements

This book has come to fruition thanks to a team of collaborators. Our first thoughts go to Roy Gionfriddo, Jeannie's husband and Mark's father, who was always there for us, continually supporting our many endeavors, and who passed before this book was completed.

Tina Gionfriddo Fleischer used her innate talent and impeccable skills to edit this book. Chrissa Lindahl aided in collecting photo images. Erica Moretti helped with Italian phrases and their translations. A special thank you goes to our friend and artist Jack McQuaide who helped design the cover for this project.

We are grateful to Paul Cohen and Colin Rolfe at Epigraph for their input and assistance, to Amy Martin for recommending Epigraph to us, and to Mark G. Auerbach at MAPR for organizing our public relations. Also, we thank author Cindy B. for helping Jeannie find her "voice" years ago, in the beginning of this labor of love. She gave her wonderful suggestions and boosted her confidence in writing.

Lastly, we want to thank Hart-Lester Harris Allen, whom we think of daily and miss so very much, for the many hours of fascinating interviews. Dear Hart... it is with great pride that we have finally kept our promise!
-JG & MG

Notes

Chapter 1
P. 8 "mother was a 1883 graduate of Smith..." Smith College Catalog 1875-1918, 93.
P. 9 "flu pandemic..." Wikipedia, 1918 Flu Pandemic

Chapter 2
P. 12 "Somerville..." *Yankee Magazine*, November 1975, Curt Norris, 119.
P. 12 "Parma Italy..." *New York Times*, January 19, 1949.
P. 13 "fruit peddler..." *Yankee Magazine*, November 1975, Curt Norris, 117.
P. 14 "two hundred dollars..." *Yankee Magazine*, November 1975, Curt Norris, 117.
P. 20 "larger quarters located on School Street..." *Yankee Magazine* November 1975 Curt Norris 118.
P. 20 "shoveled piles of money into laundry baskets..." *Yankee Magazine*, November 1975, Curt Norris 118.

Chapter 5
P. 33 "cream colored limousine..." *Yankee Magazine*, November 1975, Curt Norris, 212.
P. 35 "palatial residence..." *Literary Digest*, August 1921, Personal Glimpses.

CHAPTER 7
P. 46 "face value of almost $15,000,000..." *Yankee Magazine*, November 1975, Curt Norris, 119.
P. 52 "happiest moments of our lives..." *Yankee Magazine*, November 1975, Curt Norris, 119.

CHAPTER 8
P. 54 "Nantucket is an Indian word for Far Away Land..." *A Camera Impression*, Chamberlain, Foreword, 4.

CHAPTER 9
P. 60 "hot dogs and coffee..." *New York Times*, July 29, 1920.
P. 60 "pose for movies..." S*pringfield Evening News*, August 2, 5, 1920, 2.

CHAPTER 10
P. 68 "candidate for Governor..." *Yankee Magazine*, November 1975, Curt Norris, 112.

CHAPTER 13
P. 82 "more agents were hired..." *Yankee Magazine*, November 1975, Curt Norris, 119.
P. 83 "a cigar someone had named after him..." *Yankee Magazine*, November 1975, Curt Norris, 114.
P. 87 "I can lay my hands on $7,500,000..." *Springfield Evening News*, August 30, 1920, 1.
P. 88 "the greatest Italian that ever lived..." *Springfield Evening News*, August 3, 1920, 3.

CHAPTER 14

P. 94 "for weeks the Boston Post had been suspicious..." *Yankee Magazine*, November 1975, Curt Norris, 2.

P. 97 "Skinner satin manufactured in Holyoke..." *The Story of Holyoke*, Wyatt E. Harper, 101.

Chapter 15

P. 100 "Why not stop the farce?" *Boston News Bureau Literary Digest*, August 21, 1920, Personal Glimpses.

P. 101 "All of Boston is get rich quick mad..." *New York Evening World Literary Digest*. August 21, 1920.

P. 105 "My family was well to do..." *Literary Digest*.

P. 108 "You remember the old rube who saw a giraffe..." *Literary Digest*, August 21, 1920, Personal Glimpses.

Chapter 16

P. 113 "McMaster's article appeared on the front page..." *Yankee Magazine*, November 1975, Curt Norris, 214.

P. 113 "five million suit against the Post..." *Literary Digest*, August 21,1920, Personal Glimpses.

Chapter 17

P. 120 "Under the authority vested in me..." *Springfield Evening News*, August 11, 1920, 1.

P. 122 "there may be a contract out on my life..." *Springfield Evening News*, June, 1925.

Charter 21

P. 144 "Old Colony closes..." *Springfield Evening News* August 13, 1920, 1.

P. 144 "Polish Industrial Association..." *Springfield Evening News*, August 14, 1920, 1.

P. 144 "accounts to Lucy Martelli..." *Springfield Evening News*, August 9, 1920, 1.

P. 145 "Governor Calvin Coolidge has just made the following statement..." *Springfield Evening News*, August 12, 1920.

P. 146 "came upon Andrew Lapardo..." *Springfield Evening News*, August 11, 1920, 2.

P. 147 "Domestic and Foreign Securities and Trading..." *Springfield Evening News*, August 13, 1920, 1.

P. 147 "manager Gaetano Cataldo..." *Springfield Evening News*, August 14, 1920, 1.

CHAPTER 22

P. 149 "No extensive sales of International Reply Coupons..." *Yankee Magazine*, November 1975, Curt Norris, 212.

P. 152 "except for the moustache..." *Yankee Magazine*, November 1975, Curt Norris, 214.

P. 152 "discovered several problems..." *Yankee Magazine,* November 1975, Curt Norris, 214.

P. 153 "also known as Charles Bianchi..." *Springfield Evening News*, August 11, 1920, 1.

P. 155 "society owes me a chance..." *New York Times*, August 12, 1920, 3.

CHAPTER 23

P. 157 "head of Old Colony admitted insolvent..." *Springfield Evening News*, August 13, 1920, 1.

P. 157 "let us have Ponzi and Brightwell..." *Springfield Evening News*, August 14, 1920, 1.

P. 158 "went to the Federal Building..." *Springfield Evening News*, August 12, 1920, 1.

P. 158 "Bonds of $25,000..." *Springfield Evening News*, August 12, 1920, 1.
P. 159 "out of city for the night..." *Springfield Evening News*, August 14, 1920, 8.
P. 160 "gaze fell upon the calendar..." August 14, 1920, 8

CHAPTER 24
P. 162 "staff of accountants..." *Springfield Evening News*, August 14, 1920, 8.
P. 163 "Italian couple walked in..." *Springfield Evening News*, August 14, 1920, 8.
P. 163 "two thirds of the Boston Police Department..." *New York Times*, November 22, 1922.

CHAPTER 25
P. 166 "$40,000 mansion..." *Springfield Evening News*, January 11, 1921.
P. 166 "Ponzi's personal belongings..." *Springfield Evening News*, October 27, 1921.
P. 166 "behalf of his friend Simon Swig..." *New York Times*, November 23, 1922.
P. 167 "six months ago Charles Ponzi ate caviar..." *New York Times*, December 27, 1920.
P. 168 "Charles Ponzi - Plymouth, Massachusetts..." *New York Times*, December 23, 1920.

CPSIA information can be obtained
at www.ICGtesting.com
Printed in the USA
BVOW03*1928041116
466982BV00001B/1/P

9 781944 037345